SELMA LAGERLÖF (1858-1940) was born on a farm in Värmland, trained as a teacher and became, in her life-time, Sweden's most widely translated author ever. Novels such as *Gösta Berlings saga* (1891; *Gösta Berling's Saga*) and *Jerusalem* (1901-02) helped regenerate Swedish literature, and the school reader, *Nils Holgersson's Wonderful Journey through Sweden* (1906-07), has achieved enduring international fame and popularity. Two very different trilogies, the Löwensköld trilogy (1925-28) and the Mårbacka trilogy (1922-32), the latter often taken to be autobiographical, give some idea of the range and power of Lagerlöf's writing. Several of her texts inspired innovative films, among them *Herr Arnes pengar* (*Sir Arne's Treasure*), directed by Mauritz Stiller (1919) and based on *Herr Arnes penningar* (1903; *Lord Arne's Silver*), and *Körkarlen* (*The Phantom Carriage*), directed by Victor Sjöström (1921) and based on Lagerlöf's *Körkarlen* (1912). She was awarded the Nobel Prize for Literature, as the first woman ever, in 1909, and elected to the Swedish Academy, again as the first woman, in 1914. Having been able to buy back the farm of Mårbacka, which her family had lost as the result of bankruptcy, Lagerlöf spent the last three decades of her life combining her writing with the responsibilities for running a sizeable estate. Her work has been translated into close to 50 languages.

PETER GRAVES has translated works by Linnaeus, Jacob Wallenberg, August Strindberg, Selma Lagerlöf and Peter Englund, and he has been awarded a number of translation prizes. Before retiring he was Head of the School of Literatures, Languages and Cultures at the University of Edinburgh, where he taught Swedish.

Some other books from Norvik Press

Victoria Benedictsson: *Money* (translated by Sarah Death)

Fredrika Bremer: *The Colonel's Family* (translated by Sarah Death)

Camilla Collett: *The District Governor's Daughters* (translated by Kirsten Seaver)

Vigdis Hjorth: *A House in Norway* (translated by Charlotte Barslund)

Svava Jakobsdóttir: *Gunnlöth's Tale* (translated by Oliver Watts)

Selma Lagerlöf: *The Löwensköld Ring* (translated by Linda Schenck)
Selma Lagerlöf: *Charlotte Löwensköld* (translated by Linda Schenck)
Selma Lagerlöf: *Anna Svärd* (translated by Linda Schenck)
Selma Lagerlöf: *Lord Arne's Silver* (translated by Sarah Death)
Selma Lagerlöf: *Nils Holgersson's Wonderful Journey through Sweden* (translated by Peter Graves)
Selma Lagerlöf: *The Phantom Carriage* (translated by Peter Graves)
Selma Lagerlöf: *A Manor House Tale* (translated by Peter Graves)
Selma Lagerlöf: *Mårbacka* (translated by Sarah Death)

Klaus Rifbjerg: *Terminal Innocence* (translated by Paul Larkin)

Amalie Skram: *Fru Inés* (translated by Katherine Hanson and Judith Messick)
Amalie Skram: *Lucie* (translated by Katherine Hanson and Judith Messick)

Edith Södergran: *The Poet Who Created Herself: Selected Letters of Edith Södergran* (translated by Silvester Mazzarella)

Kirsten Thorup: *The God of Chance* (translated by Janet Garton)

Dorrit Willumsen: *Bang: A Novel about the Danish Writer* (translated by Marina Allemano)

Elin Wägner: *Penwoman* (translated by Sarah Death)

The Emperor of Portugallia
A Story from Värmland

by

Selma Lagerlöf

Translated from the Swedish
and with an
Afterword by Peter Graves

Series Preface by Helena Forsås-Scott

Norvik Press
2017

Originally published as *Kejsarn av Portugallien* in 1914.

This translation and afterword © Peter Graves 2017.
Series preface © Helena Forsås-Scott 2015.
The translator's moral right to be identified as the translator of the work has been asserted.

Norvik Press Series B: English Translations of Scandinavian Literature, no. 76

ISBN: 978-1-909408-45-6

Norvik Press gratefully acknowledges the generous support of Svenska Akademien (The Swedish Academy) towards the publication of this translation.

Norvik Press
Department of Scandinavian Studies
UCL
Gower Street
London WC1E 6BT
United Kingdom
Website: www.norvikpress.com
E-mail address: norvik.press@ucl.ac.uk

Managing editors: Elettra Carbone, Sarah Death, Janet Garton, C. Claire Thomson.

Cover design: Marita Fraser
Cover image : Elias Martin (1739 - 1818) *Romantiskt landskap med gran* (*Romantic Landscape with Spruce*)
Painting. (1768 - 1780). National Museum Stockholm.

Contents

III.

IV.

Series Preface

In the first comprehensive biography of the Swedish author Selma Lagerlöf (1858-1940), Elin Wägner provided a snapshot of her at the age of 75 that gives some idea of the range of her achievements and duties. Sitting at her desk in the library at Mårbacka with its collection of classics from Homer to Ibsen, Lagerlöf is also able to view several shelves of translations of her books. Behind her she has not only her own works and studies of herself but also a number of wooden trays into which her mail is sorted. And the trays have labels: 'Baltic Countries, Belgium, Holland, Denmark, Norway, England, France, Italy, Finland, Germany, Sweden, Switzerland, the Slavic Countries, Austria-Hungary, Bonnier [her Swedish publisher], Langen [her German publisher], Swedish Academy, the Press, Relatives and Friends, Treasures, Mårbacka Oatmeal, Miscellaneous Duties'. Lagerlöf's statement, made to her biographer Elin Wägner a few years previously, that she had at least contributed to attracting tourists to her native province of Värmland, was clearly made tongue in cheek.

How could Selma Lagerlöf, a woman born into a middle-class family in provincial Sweden around the middle of the nineteenth century, produce such an œuvre (sixteen novels, seven volumes of short stories) and achieve such status and fame in her lifetime?

Growing up on Mårbacka, a farm in the province of Värmland, at a time when the Swedish economy was predominantly agricultural, Selma Lagerlöf and her sisters learnt about the tasks necessary to keep the self-sufficient household ticking over, but their opportunities of getting an education beyond that which could be provided by their governess were close to non-existent. Selma Lagerlöf succeeded in borrowing money to spend three years in Stockholm training to become a teacher, one of the few professions open to women at the time, and after qualifying in 1885 she spent ten years teaching at a junior high school for girls in Landskrona, in the south of Sweden. Mårbacka had to be sold at auction in 1888, and Lagerlöf only resigned from her teaching post four years after the publication of her first novel, establishing herself as a writer in a Sweden quite different from the one in which she had grown up. Industrialisation in Sweden was late but swift, and Lagerlöf's texts found new readers among the urban working class.

Lagerlöf remained a prolific author well into the 1930s, publishing chiefly novels and short stories as well as a textbook for school children, and she soon also gained recognition in the form of honours and prizes: an Honorary Doctorate at the University of Uppsala in 1907, the Nobel Prize for Literature, as the first woman, in 1909, and election to the Swedish Academy, again as the first woman, in 1914. Suffrage for women was only introduced in Sweden in 1919, and Lagerlöf became a considerable asset to the campaign. She was also able to repurchase Mårbacka, including the farm land, and from 1910 onwards she combined her work as a writer with responsibility for a sizeable estate with a considerable number of employees.

To quote Lagerlöf's most recent biographer, Vivi Edström, she 'knew how to tell a story without ruining it'; but her innovative literary language with its close affinity with spoken language required hard work and much experimentation. 'We authors', Lagerlöf wrote in a letter in 1908, 'regard a book as close to completion once we have found the style in which it allows itself to be written'.

Her first novel, *Gösta Berlings saga* (1891; *Gösta Berling's Saga*), was indeed a long time in the making as Lagerlöf experimented with genres and styles before settling for an exuberant and inventive form of prose fiction that is richly intertextual and frequently addresses the reader. Set in Värmland in the 1820s with the young and talented Gösta Berling as the hero, the narrative celebrates the parties, balls and romantic adventures throughout 'the year of the cavaliers' at the iron foundry of Ekeby. But it does so against the backdrop of the expulsion of the Major's Wife who has been benefactress of the cavaliers; and following her year-long pilgrimage and what has effectively been a year of misrule by the cavaliers, it is hard work and communal responsibility that emerge as the foundations of the future.

In *Drottningar i Kungahälla* (1899; *The Queens of Kungahälla*) Lagerlöf brought together a series of short stories and an epic poem set in Viking-age Kungälv, some distance north of Gothenburg, her aim being to explore some of the material covered by the medieval Icelandic author Snorri Sturluson in *Heimskringla*, but from the perspectives of the female characters. The terse narrative of *Herr Arnes penningar* (1903; *Lord Arne's Silver*), set in the sixteenth century in a context that reinforces boundary crossings and ambivalences, has a plot revolving around murder and robbery, ghosts, love and eventual punishment. The slightly earlier short novel *En herrgårdssägen* (1899; *A Manor House Tale*) similarly transcends boundaries as it explores music and dreams, madness and sanity, death and life in the context of the emerging relationship between a young woman and man.

A few lines in a newspaper inspired Lagerlöf to her biggest literary project since *Gösta Berlings Saga*, the two-volume novel *Jerusalem* (1901-02), which also helped pave the way for her Nobel Prize later in the decade. The plot launches straight into the topic of emigration, widespread in Sweden since the 1860s, by exploring a farming community in the province of Dalarna and the emigration of part of the community to Jerusalem. The style was inspired by the medieval Icelandic sagas, but although the focus on emigration also established a thematic link with the sagas, the inversions of saga patterns such as bloody confrontations and family feuds become more prominent as the plot foregrounds peaceful achievements and international understanding. Yet this is first and foremost a narrative in which traditional structures of stability are torn apart, in which family relationships and relations between lovers are tried and often found wanting, and in which the eventual reconciliation between old and new comes at a considerable price.

Lagerlöf had been commissioned to write a school reader in 1901, but it was several years before she hit on the idea of presenting the geography, economy, history and culture of the provinces of Sweden through the story of a young boy criss-crossing the country on the back of a goose. While working on *Nils Holgerssons underbara resa genom Sverige* (1906-07; *Nils Holgersson's Wonderful Journey*), Lagerlöf doubted that the text would find readers outside Sweden; paradoxically, however, *Nils Holgersson* was to become her greatest international success. Once perceived as an obstacle to the ambitions to award Lagerlöf the Nobel Prize for Literature, *Nils Holgersson* is nowadays read as a complex and innovative novel.

Körkarlen (1912; *The Phantom Carriage*) grew out of a request from The National Tuberculosis Society, and what was intended as a short story soon turned into a novel. The story of a victim of TB, whose death on New Year's Eve destines him to drive the death cart throughout the following year and who only gains the respite to atone for his failures and omissions thanks to the affection and love of others, became the basis in 1921 for one of the best-known Swedish films of the silent era, with Victor Sjöström as the director (Sjöström also played the central character) and with ground-breaking cinematography by J. Julius (Julius Jaenzon).

The First World War was a difficult time for Lagerlöf: while many of her readers, in Sweden and abroad, were expecting powerful statements against the war, she felt that the political events were draining her creative powers. *Kejsarn av Portugallien* (1914; *The Emperor of Portugallia*) is not just a novel about the miracle of a newborn child and a father's love of his daughter; it is also a text about a fantasy world emerging in response to extreme external pressures, and about the insights and support this seemingly mad world can generate. Jan, the central character, develops for himself an outsider position similar to that occupied by Sven Elversson in Lagerlöf's more emphatically pacifist novel *Bannlyst*

(1918; *Banished*), a position that allows for both critical and innovative perspectives on society.

Quite different from Lagerlöf's wartime texts, the trilogy consisting of *Löwensköldska ringen* (1925; *The Löwensköld Ring*), *Charlotte Löwensköld* (1925) and *Anna Svärd* (1928) is at once lighthearted and serious, a narrative tour de force playing on ambivalences and multiple interpretations to an extent that has the potential to destabilise, in retrospect, any hard and fast readings of Lagerlöf's œuvre. As the trilogy calls into question the ghost of the old warrior General Löwensköld and then traces the demise of Karl-Artur Ekenstedt, a promising young minister in the State Lutheran Church, while giving prominence to a series of strong and independent female characters, the texts explore and celebrate the capacity and power of narrative.

Lagerlöf wrote another trilogy late in her career, and one that has commonly been regarded as autobiographical: *Mårbacka* (1922), *Ett barns memoarer* (1930; *Memories of My Childhood*), and *Dagbok för Selma Ottilia Lovisa Lagerlöf* (1932; *The Diary of Selma Lagerlöf*). All three are told in the first person; and with their tales about the Lagerlöfs, relatives, friends, local characters and the activities that structured life at Mårbacka in the 1860s and 70s, the first two volumes can certainly be read as evoking storytelling in the family circle by the fire in the evening. The third volume, *Diary*, was initially taken to be the authentic diary of a fourteen-year-old Selma Lagerlöf. Birgitta Holm's psychoanalytical study of Lagerlöf's work (1984) reads the Mårbacka trilogy in innovative terms and singles out *Diary* as providing the keys to Lagerlöf's œuvre. Ulla-Britta Lagerroth has interpreted the trilogy as a gradual unmasking of patriarchy; but with 'Selma Lagerlöf' at its centre, this work can also be read as a wide-ranging and playful exploration of gender, writing and fame.

With the publication over the past couple of decades of several volumes of letters by Lagerlöf, to her friend Sophie Elkan (1994), to her mother (1998), to her friend and assistant Valborg Olander (2006), and to her friends Anna Oom and Elise Malmros (2009-10), our understanding of Lagerlöf has undoubtedly become more complex. While the focus of much of the early research on Lagerlöf's work was biographical, several Swedish studies centring on the texts were published in connection with the centenary of her birth in 1958. A new wave of Lagerlöf scholarship began to emerge in Sweden in the late 1990s, exploring areas such narrative, gender, genre, and aesthetics; and in the 1990s the translation, reception and impact of Lagerlöf's texts abroad became an increasingly important field, investigated by scholars in for example the US, the UK and Japan as well as in Sweden. Current research is expanding into the interrelations between media in Lagerlöf, performance studies, cultural transmissions, and archival studies. As yet there is no scholarly edition of Lagerlöf, but thanks to the newly established Selma Lagerlöf Archive (Selma Lagerlöf-arkivet, accessible at litteraturbanken.se) a scholarly edition in digitised form is underway. Three works were completed by 2013: *Gösta Berling's saga*, *Osynliga länkar* and *Körkarlen*.

By the time Lagerlöf turned 80, in 1938, she was the most widely translated Swedish writer ever, and the total number of languages into which her work has been translated is now close to 50. However, most of the translations into English were made soon after the appearance of the original Swedish texts, and unlike the original texts, translations soon become dated. Moreover, as Peter Graves has concluded in a study of Lagerlöf in Britain, Lagerlöf 'was not well-served by her translators [into English]'. 'Lagerlöf in English', a series of new translations launched in 2011, aims to remedy this situation.

Helena Forsås-Scott
(1945-2015. First editor of the 'Lagerlöf in English' series.)

A list of further reading can be found at the end of the Translator's Afterword at the back of this volume.

I.

The Beating Heart

However old he grew, Jan Andersson at Skrolycka never tired of telling of the day his little girl came into the world.

He had gone to fetch the midwife and other helpers early in the morning, after which he had spent the rest of the morning and a good part of the afternoon sitting on the chopping block in the woodshed with nothing to do but wait.

It was raining outside, lashing down, and he got his share of it even though he was sitting under what passed as a roof. The damp penetrated the walls and got to him, and drips from the leaky roof found him, and the wind blew torrents in on him since the woodshed had a doorway but no door.

'I wonder if anyone actually believes I'm happy about the arrival of this child,' he muttered to himself and suddenly kicked a stick so hard that it flew out across the yard. 'It's just about the worst misfortune that could have happened to me. When we married, Kattrinna and me, it was because we were sick and tired of being farmhand and maid over at Erik's place at Falla Farm and wanted to get our feet under a table of our own. It certainly wasn't because we wanted children.'

Putting his head in his hands he gave a deep sigh. Of course the cold and the damp and the long, tedious wait were lowering his spirits, but there was a lot more to it than that. There was a profoundly serious aspect to his concerns.

'Work,' he thought, 'I have to work from morning to night every single day, but at least I have some peace at night. So far. But now there will be a crying baby and I won't even be able to rest at night.'

His despair deepened at the thought and he wrung his

hands so hard that his knuckles cracked.

'Everything has gone well for the two of us because Kattrinna has been able to go out to work, the same as me. But now she'll have to stay at home and look after the child.'

His gaze became dark and gloomy as if he could see the figure of Famine creeping across the yard and forcing its way into the cottage.

'I'll tell it as it is,' he said, slamming his fist down on the chopping block as if to drive home his words, 'if only I'd known back when Erik at Falla came and offered me some scrap timber to build a cottage for myself on his land, if only I'd known it would turn out like this, I'd rather have said no to the lot of it and carried on living in the farmhands' bothy at Falla for the rest of my days.'

They were strong words, he knew that, but he was in no mood to take them back.

'If something happened ...' he began, because now he had reached the point of wanting to say he would have no objection if some misfortune were to befall the child before it even came into the world. But he had no time to finish the thought before it was interrupted by the soft sound of a baby's cry through the wall.

The woodshed was built on to the cottage and when he listened he could hear one cry after another from inside. He knew at once what this meant and he sat silently for some time, showing neither joy nor sorrow. A last he gave a slight shrug.

'Well, it's here,' he said, 'and now surely to God I can be allowed indoors to warm myself up a bit?'

But comfort and relief were in no hurry to come and he found himself still sitting waiting as the hours passed.

The rain continued to pour down as before, but the wind grew stronger and although it was the beginning of August it felt as raw as a November day.

As if all that wasn't enough, another thought occurred to him and made him even more miserable. He began to feel undervalued and neglected.

'Not counting the midwife, there are three women in there

with Kattrinna,' he muttered. 'One of them could at least have taken the trouble to come and tell me whether it's a boy or a girl.'

As he sat there he could hear them making up the fire in the stove and he could see them going out to the spring for water, but he might as well not have existed as far as they were concerned.

He put his head in his hands and began rocking backwards and forwards.

'Tell me this, Jan Andersson,' he said, 'just tell me this. What is the matter with you? Why does everything you do go so badly? Why is your life so dull and tedious? Why on earth couldn't you have married a pretty young thing instead of old Kattrinna, the cowmaid at Falla?'

He was utterly miserable, so much so that tears trickled between his fingers.

'Why does the parish hold you in such low regard? Can you say why, Jan Andersson? Why are you always pushed aside? You know there are others just as poor as you, just as frail when it comes to work, but not one of them is passed over like you are. So what is the matter with you, just tell me that, Jan Andersson?'

It was a question he had often asked himself without ever finding an answer. And he probably didn't expect to find the answer this time, either. Come to that, perhaps there wasn't anything the matter with him? Perhaps the truth was that both God and his fellow beings really were treating him unjustly?

With that thought in mind he raised his head from his hands and tried to put a brave face on it.

'If you are ever allowed back into your cottage, Jan Andersson, my lad,' he said, 'you won't as much as look at that baby. You'll just walk straight over to the stove and warm yourself up without saying a word.

'Or maybe you should just leave! No need for you to sit here any longer now you know the baby's born. Why not just show Kattrinna and the other womenfolk what you're made of ...'

He was just about to get up when the farmer's wife appeared

17

at the woodshed door. She gave a nice curtsey and asked him to come in and see the baby.

Given the mood he was in, if it had not been the farmer's wife herself who invited him he might well not have gone, angry as he was. As it was, he followed her, though he certainly didn't hurry. He did his best to adopt the same gait and demeanour that the big farmer, Erik of Falla Farm, used when walking across the parish hall to put his voting slip in the ballot box. And he actually made quite a good job of imitating that look of surly solemnity.

'Do come in, Jan,' the mistress of Falla Farm said, opening the cottage door for him and stepping aside to allow him to go in first.

He saw at once that everything had been cleaned and tidied. The coffee pot was standing cooling on the slab by the stove and the table in the window was laid with a snow-white tablecloth and coffee cups from Falla Farm. Kattrinna lay in bed and the two other women who had been there to help were standing back against the wall to give him a clear view of all the arrangements.

In front of the coffee table stood the midwife, holding a bundle in her arms.

He couldn't help thinking that it looked – for once – as if he was the centre of attention. Kattrinna was looking at him with a gentle expression that seemed to be asking whether he was pleased with her. All the others had their eyes on him and looked as if they were waiting for him to praise the efforts they had made on his behalf.

But it is not that easy to be happy when you have spent the whole day freezing and angry outside. He found he could not wipe Erik's expression off his face and he stood there without saying a word.

Then the midwife stepped forward. The cottage was so small that a single step was enough to bring her right up to him and she passed the baby into his arms.

'Just take a look at the little girl, Jan ... she's perfect!' she said.

So he found himself holding something warm and soft and wrapped in a large shawl. The shawl was folded back enough for him to see a small creased face and tiny wrinkled hands. As he stood there wondering what the womenfolk expected him to do with this bundle the midwife had put in his arms, he felt a sudden shock, strong enough to make both him and the baby jump. It had nothing to do with the others present, and it was impossible for him to tell whether it passed from the little girl to him or from him to the little girl.

And his heart immediately began to throb as it had never done before, and all at once he was no longer frozen and no longer miserable and worried and no longer angry. Everything was good. The only thing that did concern him was that he couldn't understand why his heart should be pounding and hammering so hard when he hadn't been dancing or running or climbing a steep hill.

'Please,' he said to the midwife, 'please put your hand here and feel my heart. It's beating so strangely.'

'It really is pounding,' the midwife said. 'Perhaps it does that from time to time?'

'I've never had it before,' he assured her. 'Never like this.'

'Do you feel unwell? Does it hurt?'

No, nothing like that.

Since the midwife couldn't understand what was wrong with him, she said: 'I'd better take the baby just in case.'

But then Jan felt that he didn't want to hand over the baby.

'No,' he said. 'Leave the little one with me!'

That is when the women must have read something in his eyes or heard something in his voice. Whatever it was it made them happy, for the midwife gave a little smile and the other women actually laughed out loud.

'Jan, have you never ever liked someone so much that it has made your heart race?' the midwife asked.

'No ... no,' Jan said hesitantly.

At that moment he understood what had made his heart beat so. And more than that, he began to realise what had been wrong with him throughout his life. For someone who cannot feel the workings of sorrow or joy in his heart truly cannot yet be considered a full human being.

Klara Fina Goldenborg

The following day Jan stood at the cottage door for several hours. He had the little girl in his arms.

This time, too, he had a long wait, but everything was very different from the day before. The companion he had with him now was so good that nothing could make him weary or downcast.

He couldn't describe how good it felt to hold this warm little body close to him. He felt that up to now he had been bitter and nasty even to himself, but now he was all sweetness and bliss. He had never known that truly loving someone else could bring such delight.

He was not standing in the doorway for no reason at all, of course, and while standing there he was hoping that a matter of great importance would be decided.

He and Kattrinna had spent the whole morning trying to choose a name for the child. In spite of hours of long, hard thinking, they still couldn't reach a decision.

'I can't see any other solution than for you to take the baby and stand at the door with her,' Kattrinna had said eventually. 'You can ask the name of the first woman who passes and whatever name she says we will give the baby, whether it's rough or elegant.'

As it happens, however, their cottage was rather isolated and people did not walk past very often. Jan found himself standing in the doorway for a long time without anyone going by. It was an overcast day, but it wasn't raining, nor was it windy or cold – in fact it was rather muggy.

If it had not been for the little girl in his arms Jan would quickly have despaired of the whole business.

'Jan Andersson, my good fellow,' he would have said to himself, 'have you forgotten that you live in the back of beyond, by Lake Duvsjön in Askedalarna where there is only one decent farm and all the rest are fishermen's huts and cottars' hovels? No one round here is likely to have a nice enough name for you to want to give it to your little girl.'

But since it was all about his daughter, Jan had no doubt that things would turn out well. He stood there looking down along the lake, which lay in the hollow between the hills, and chose not to see how isolated from the rest of the district it was. After all, one of the gentry with a fine name might come rowing up from the Duvnäs estate at the southern end of the lake? It might happen, mightn't it? And, for the little girl's sake, he was almost sure that was what would happen.

The baby slept the whole time so it didn't matter how long he chose to stand and wait. But Kattrinna was more difficult and she kept asking whether anyone was coming and telling him he shouldn't stay out with the baby any longer.

Jan raised his eyes and surveyed Storsnipa, the hill that towered like a bastion above the small fields and scraps of arable land in Askedalarna and kept strangers at bay. It was just possible, he thought, that some fine ladies had gone up the hill to enjoy the wonderful view. And they might get lost on the way down and come past Skrolycka.

He calmed Kattrinna down as well as he could. There was nothing the matter with either him or the baby and since he had been standing there so long he was quite happy to stay there a while longer.

There was no sign of anyone, but he was certain that all he had to do was to be patient and help would come. It was bound to. It would not have surprised him if a queen in a golden coach had come driving through the hills and woods just to pass on her name to the little girl.

More time passed. He realised that evening was approaching and he wouldn't be able to stay there much longer.

In the cottage Kattrinna could see the time and began again to ask him to come indoors.

'Just be patient for a while,' he said. 'I think I can see

something over in the west.'

It had been cloudy all day, but just at that moment the sun broke through the clouds and its rays fell upon the baby.

'I'm not in the least surprised that you want to take a look at the little girl before you go down,' Jan said to the sun. 'She is worth looking at, I can tell you.'

The sun broke through even more brightly and spread a golden glow over the baby and the cottage.

'Do you want to be her godmother, is that it?' Jan said.

The sun made no answer but she shone bright and red again. Then she covered herself with a veil of cloud and disappeared.

That is when Kattrinna spoke again. 'Was there someone there? I thought I heard you talking to someone. You really do have to come in now.'

'Yes, I'm coming,' Jan said and immediately went indoors. 'That was a very fine gentlewoman who went past. She was in such a hurry I barely had time to say "Good day" before she was gone.'

'Oh, mercy me! That really is annoying, seeing as how long we've been waiting. Surely you had time to ask her what she was called?'

'Yes I did. Her name was Klara Fina Goldenborg, I got that much out of her.'

'Klara Fina Goldenborg! Surely that's too grand a name?' Kattrinna said, but made no further comment.

Jan, however, was quite amazed at himself for having come up with such a wonderful idea as choosing the sun to be the baby's godmother. The fact is, he had become a different man from the moment the little girl was put in his arms.

The Christening

When the time came for the little girl from Skrolycka to be christened, her father Jan behaved so foolishly that both Kattrinna and the godparents ended up giving him a scolding.

The child was to be carried to the font by the wife of Erik, the Falla farmer, and she rode to the manse with the little girl in her arms while Erik himself walked alongside the cart, leading the horse. The stretch of the road to Duvnäs ironworks was so poor that it could scarcely be called a road and Erik was intent on being careful since he was conveying a child as yet unbaptised.

Jan watched them depart. He had brought the baby from the cottage himself and no one knew better than him what fine people they were into whose care he was entrusting the baby. He knew that Erik was as competent as a driver as he was at everything else, and he knew that the farmer's wife had borne and raised seven children. So he had no reason to feel the slightest concern.

Once they had left, however, and Jan had gone back to ditching one of Erik's fallow fields, a terrible anxiety overwhelmed him. What if Erik's horse bolted? What if the minister were to drop the baby when taking her from her godmother? What if the farmer's wife wrapped the little girl in so many shawls that she was smothered by the time they arrived at the manse?

He told himself there was no need to be so worried – after all, it was Erik and his wife who were the godparents. But his worries would not go away and without further ado he put down his spade and set off for the manse in the clothes he stood up in. He took the short cut over the hill and moved so quickly that when Erik drove into the minister's stableyard Jan Andersson from Skrolycka was the first thing he caught sight of.

It is not at all proper, as we know, for the mother and father to be present when a child is baptised and Jan could see at once that the Falla farmer and his wife were displeased that he had come running to the manse. Erik unhitched the horse himself without waving him over to help, and Erik's wife lifted the baby high in her arms and walked across the yard to the manse and into the kitchen without saying a word to Jan.

Since the godparents clearly did not want to acknowledge his presence, Jan didn't dare approach them. But he did hear a little squeak from the bundle of shawls as the farmer's wife walked past, so at least he knew that the baby had not been smothered on the way.

He knew himself that it was stupid not to return home immediately, but he was now so convinced the minister would drop the baby that he felt he had to stay.

He waited in the stableyard for a while, then he went up to the house and into the hall.

There is nothing more unseemly than the father accompanying the party to the minister's, especially when the child's godparents are people like Erik from Falla Farm and his wife. When the door to the minister's office opened and Jan Andersson, still in his filthy working clothes, slipped into the room just after the minister had started the service, thus making it impossible for them to eject the intruder, both godparents swore to themselves that the moment they got home they would give him a piece of their minds about how badly he had behaved.

The christening passed off just as it should and there wasn't the slightest sign of an accident. Jan Andersson's intrusion proved utterly unnecessary and just before the service finished he opened the door and slipped quietly back out into the hall. By then it was obvious even to him that everything was going well without him.

A little while later Erik and his wife also came out into the hall. They were on their way to the kitchen, which was where Erik's wife had removed and left all the baby's shawls.

Farmer Erik went on ahead to open the kitchen door for his wife, but just as he was doing so, two kittens came scampering into the hall. They tumbled over one another right in front of the farmer's wife so that she tripped and was on the point of falling headlong. The thought was just running through her mind, 'I am going to fall with the baby and it will die and I shall be unhappy for the rest of my life' when a strong hand grabbed her and held her up. On turning to look she discovered that her helper was none other than Jan Andersson, who had waited in the hall as if knowing that was the place where he would be needed.

Before she had time to gather her thoughts and say anything to him, he was gone. And when she and her husband Erik arrived home, Jan was already back working at the ditching.

He had sensed that once that moment of danger was behind him, he could safely return home.

Neither Farmer Erik nor his wife said anything to him about the unseemliness of his behaviour. Instead, the farmer's wife invited him in for coffee just as he was, streaked with mud from his autumn work on the waterlogged fallow field.

Vaccination

When the time came for the little girl from Skrolycka to be vaccinated, no one questioned the fact that Jan, her father, would go too, that being what he wanted. The vaccination was to be done one evening in late August and it was already so dark when Kattrinna left home that she was glad to have someone there to help her over stiles and ditches and all the other obstacles along the badly-made track.

The vaccination session was being held at Falla Farm and Erik's wife had built the fire up so high that she obviously thought there was no need to provide any other lighting except for a slim candle placed on the small table where the cantor would do his work.

The Skrolycka folk, like everyone else who was there, thought the room was unusually bright. In spite of that, however, the walls of the room still lay in a gloomy, grey darkness that made the room seem smaller than it actually was, and in this dark area it was just possible to pick out a crowd of women with children no more than a year old, all of whom had to be carried, rocked, fed and cared for in every way imaginable.

Most of the women were unwrapping their little ones from the shawls and blankets in which they were swathed. Then they removed the children's colourful cardigans and untied the ribbons fastening their shirts to make it easier to bare the baby's upper body when the cantor called them up to the table for vaccination.

The room was remarkably quiet even though there were so many noisy little creatures gathered together in one place. They seemed to be enjoying looking at one another so much that they forgot to make a fuss. The cantor was chatting away quietly the whole time and the mothers stayed quiet in order to hear what he was saying.

'I can't think of anything nicer than going around doing the vaccinations and seeing all these beautiful babies,' the cantor said. 'Let's take a look now and see whether you've produced a good crop this year!'

He was the schoolmaster as well as cantor and he had lived in the parish his whole life. He had vaccinated the mothers, taught them, seen them confirmed and married, and now he was vaccinating their children. This was these little ones' first meeting with a man who would later play such a big part in their lives.

At first everything seemed to be going well. The mothers came forward in turn, sat on a chair by the table and held out their babies so the candle lit up their bare left arms. And while still chattering away, the cantor made three scratches in the pale white skin without the babies making a sound.

Then each mother would carry her baby over near the fire in order to dry the vaccine. Meanwhile she would be thinking about what the cantor had said about her child – that it was big and bonny and a credit to the farm, that it would be as capable as its father and its grandfather, perhaps even more so.

And that's how things proceeded, quietly and peacefully, until it came to Kattrinna's turn to sit at the vaccination table with her Klara.

The little girl simply wanted nothing to do with vaccination. She screamed and thrashed and kicked. Kattrinna hushed her, the cantor talked gently and kindly to her, but she was so frightened there was no way of controlling her.

Kattrinna had to take her away and try to calm her down. A big, strong boy was vaccinated next and he didn't make a sound, but when Kattrinna went back with the little girl there was the same fuss. She was unable to hold the baby still long enough for the cantor to make as much as a single scratch.

All of the children had been vaccinated and Klara from Skrolycka was the only one left. Kattrinna was beside herself that her baby had behaved so badly. She did not know what to do, but then Jan stepped out of the darkness by the door. He took the baby in his arms and Kattrinna rose from the chair to let him sit down.

'Go on then, you try! See if you can do any better!' she said in a slightly scornful voice, because she wasn't the kind of woman to think that the little work-worn farmhand she had married was better than her in any way.

He took the baby in his arms and Kattrinna rose from the chair to let him sit down.

But before Jan sat down he shrugged off his jerkin and it was obvious he had rolled up his shirtsleeve in the darkness, because his left arm was bare.

He really wanted to be vaccinated, that's what he said. He had only ever been vaccinated once and there was nothing in this world that frightened him as much as smallpox.

The moment the little girl saw his bare arm she went quiet and gazed at her father with big, intelligent eyes.

She watched attentively as the cantor made the three red scratches on his arm, her eyes moving from the cantor to her father, and she saw that it didn't affect him at all badly.

When it was finished, Jan Andersson turned to the cantor: 'The lass is so quiet now, perhaps you could try again?'

And the cantor did so and this time everything went well. The little girl sat the whole time with a self-possessed look on her face and didn't make a sound.

The cantor also said nothing until he had finished his work. Then he said: 'If you did that just to calm the child down, Jan, we could simply have pretended ...'

But Jan answered: 'It wouldn't have worked, I can tell you. She is one of a kind, that girl, and you'd have no chance of making her believe in something that pretends to be what it isn't.'

The Birthday

On the day of the little girl's first birthday her father Jan was digging and ditching Farmer Erik's fallow land.

He tried to remember how things used to be, back in the days when he had no one to think about when he was working on the land, back when he had never felt longing, when he had never worried, when the heart in his breast had not been beating.

'How can anyone live like that, how can they?' he said, feeling scorn for his former self.

'This,' he continued, 'this is what it all comes down to. If I were as rich as Farmer Erik or as strong as Börje who's digging the field beside me, it would be as nothing compared with having a beating heart in your breast.'

He looked over at his workmate, who was a man of enormous strength who could do almost twice the work he could do himself. And he noticed that on that particular day Börje had not managed to finish his ditching as quickly as he usually did.

They were doing piecework and Börje always contracted to do more than Jan and yet they almost always finished at about the same time. But today Börje was slow. He hadn't even kept up – in fact, he had fallen a long way behind.

Jan had been putting his back into it in order to get home to his little girl as soon as he could. He was longing to see her today even more than usual. She was sleepy in the evening and if he didn't hurry she might have fallen asleep for the night.

When Jan finished he saw that Börje had barely done half his contracted share. Not in all the years they had worked together had anything like that happened and Jan was so surprised that he went over to him.

Börje was standing down in the ditch struggling to loosen a clod of earth. He had stepped on a piece of glass and there was a deep cut on the sole of his foot. He couldn't bear wearing a boot on that foot and it's easy to imagine how painful it was to drive the spade into the ground with a cut foot.

'Aren't you going to give up?' Jan Andersson asked.

'I have to finish it today,' his companion said. 'I won't get any corn from Farmer Erik until I've finished what I'm contracted to do. And we've got no rye flour left.'

'I see. Well, goodnight to you, then,' Jan said.

Börje didn't answer. He was beyond tired and couldn't even manage the usual evening farewell.

Jan from Skrolycka walked to the edge of the field, but there he stopped.

'What does it matter to the little girl if you go home for her birthday?' he said to himself. 'She'll get on just as well without you. But Börje has seven children at home and no food to feed them. Are you going to let them go hungry so that you can go home and play with Klara Goldie?'

He set to work alongside Börje, but he was already weary so the work did not go quickly and it was almost dark before they finished.

'Klara will have been asleep for hours,' he thought as he finally shovelled his last spadeful.

'Goodnight to you!' he shouted to Börje for the second time that day.

'Goodnight,' Börje said, 'and thanks for your help. I'll go and get that rye flour immediately. And I'll help you out some other time, you can rely on that.'

'I don't want any payment. Goodnight!'

'Don't you want anything in exchange for helping me? What's got into you? Are you that posh?'

'No, not that ... it's just that it's the lass's birthday today.'

'And that's why you helped me with the ditching?'

'Yes, and there is something else as well ... Goodnight anyway!'

Jan walked away quickly in order not to be tempted to explain what the other thing was. It was on the tip of his tongue to say: 'It isn't just Klara Fina Goldenborg's birthday, it's also the birthday of my heart.'

But it was just as well he refrained from saying it because Börje might well have thought he'd gone mad.

Christmas Morning

When the little girl was sixteen months old Jan Andersson took her to church on Christmas morning.

His wife Kattrinna thought the girl was a bit young to be going to church and was afraid the child would start screaming as she had done at her vaccination. But since it was quite usual for small children to go to the early morning Christmas service with their parents, she let her husband have his own way.

They set off with their daughter at about five o'clock on Christmas morning. The sky was overcast and it was as dark as in a sack, but it wasn't cold. The air was very still and almost mild, as it often is towards the end of December.

The path they had to take at first was a small and narrow one between the ploughed fields and meadows of Askedalarna, after which they had to follow the steep winter path up over Snipaåsen ridge. Only then would they reach a proper road.

There were lights in every window of the big two-storey farmhouse at Falla and it acted as a beacon for the Skrolycka family, helping them to find Börje's cottage. There they joined up with some of their neighbours who had made torches on Christmas Eve to light their way. Each little group of people was led by a torch bearer. Most people walked in silence, but they were all in a cheerful mood. They thought of themselves as being like the three wise men, following a star in order to find the new-born King of the Jews.

At the top of the forest they had to pass a large boulder that a giant down in Frykerud had thrown at Svartsjö church one Christmas morning. Fortunately it had sailed right over the church tower and ended up lying up here on the Snipaåsen ridge. As the churchgoers approached it, the boulder was lying on the ground as usual, but they all knew that during the night it had been raised up on twelve golden pillars and the trolls had feasted and danced beneath it.

It wasn't pleasant to have to pass a boulder of that sort on Christmas morning and Jan looked over at Kattrinna to make sure she was holding the little girl tight. Kattrinna, as usual, was walking calmly and unconcernedly, chatting with a neighbour. She didn't seem to be giving any thought at all to how dangerous this place was.

The spruce trees up on the ridge were gnarled and ancient, and when you saw them in the light of the blazing torches it was impossible not to notice that many of the trees that usually looked like ordinary trees were, in fact, trolls with sharp eyes that peered out from under white, snowy hats. And they had long sharp claws protruding from gloves of heavy snow.

They had nothing to worry about as long as the trees stayed still, but what if one of them were to stretch out an arm and grab someone as they walked past? There was unlikely to be any great risk to the adults and the old folk, but Jan had always heard that trolls loved little human children, the smaller the better.

He thought the way Kattrinna was carrying their little girl was altogether too casual. It would be easy for the great claw hands of a troll to snatch the child from her, but he didn't dare take the child from her in a place as dangerous as this – that might be just the thing to set the gang of trolls in motion.

Whispers and murmurs were already spreading from one troll tree to another. Their branches were beginning to creak as though trying to make a move.

And Jan daren't risk asking his companions whether they were seeing and hearing the same things as he was. That, too, might be the sort of thing that stirred the trolls into action.

In his anxiety there was only one thing he could think of doing, which was to strike up a hymn there in the forest, and he began to sing.

Jan had a poor singing voice and he had never sung before, not so that anyone heard him, anyway. He was so bad at staying in tune that he didn't even risk singing in church, but now he had no choice, whatever it sounded like.

He could see his companions were more than a little surprised. Those walking at the front nudged one another and looked back. But he couldn't allow that to stop him, he had to carry on.

Then, almost immediately, one of the women whispered to him: 'Hang on Jan, I'll help you out.' And she began singing the Christmas hymn to the right melody and in tune.

Among the trees and in the darkness of the night it sounded so beautiful the others couldn't resist joining in: 'We greet this wondrous morningtide, by holy prophets prophesied.'

Then it was as if a murmur of fear ran through the tree trolls. They pulled their snowy hoods low so their angry troll eyes were no longer visible, and they drew in their claws beneath the spruce needles and snow. By the time the first verse faded away there was no one who could see the trees up on the forested ridge as anything other than plain, old, harmless spruce trees.

*

The flaming torches that had helped the people of Askedalarna through the forest had burnt out by the time they reached the road, but now they had the lights of farms to guide them. When one house was passing from sight, the lights of the next glittered a short way ahead. Every house had candles burning in every window to guide poor wanderers along the road to church.

At last they came to the top of a small hill from where they could see the church. There it stood like a giant lantern, with beams of light streaming out through every window. When the walkers caught sight of it, they stopped and took a deep breath. After the small cottages and low windows they had passed on their way, the church seemed so wonderfully big and so wonderfully bright.

When Jan saw the church his thoughts went straight to a poor couple in Palestine who had been on the road at night, bearing with them a little child, their only comfort and joy. They came from Bethlehem and were on their way to Jerusalem because their child was to be circumcised in the temple there. But they were compelled to travel stealthily under the cover of darkness because there were many people who were a threat to that child's life.

The people from Askedalarna had left home early in order to arrive at the church before the people in carts and carriages, but now they were being overtaken by them. With snorting horses and bells jingling, they flashed past at speed, forcing the unfortunate pedestrians to walk where the snow was deep.

By now it was Jan who was carrying the child and time after time he was forced to leap to the side. Progress along the dark road became difficult, but the bright shining temple lay before them and once they reached it they would be safe.

Then, behind them, came a great crashing of hooves and the sound of sleigh bells as a large sledge pulled by a pair of horses drew level. A young gentleman in black furs and with a tall fur hat was sitting beside his young wife. He had taken the reins himself and his coachman was standing behind him with a burning torch in his hand. He had raised it aloft and the wind blew the flame backwards, leaving a long trail of smoke and sparks in their wake.

Jan was standing up high on the roadside snowdrift, holding the child in his arms. It looked dangerous, for one of his feet suddenly sank deep into the drift and he came close to falling. The gentleman on the sledge pulled hard on the reins and shouted over to the people he had driven off the road.

'Pass the child to us and she can ride to the church with me!' he said in a friendly voice. 'It's dangerous to be carrying a little one when there is so much traffic on the road.'

'Thanks,' Jan Andersson said. 'But we'll manage fine.'

'We can have the little girl up here between us, Jan,' the young woman said.

'No thanks, we'll carry on as we are.'

35

'I see! You daren't let her out of your sight,' the young gentleman said and drove on laughing.

The walkers continued, their journey becoming more and more dangerous and difficult. Sledge followed sledge and every horse in the parish was in harness that Christmas morning.

'You could have let them take the girl,' Kattrinna said. 'I'm frightened you are going to fall over with her.'

'I should have let them take the child! Do you know what you're saying? Didn't you see who it was?'

'How could it possibly have been dangerous to let her ride with the laird of Duvnäs and his lady?'

Jan Andersson from Skrolycka came to a sudden stop. 'Was it the laird and his wife?' he said, looking as if he'd woken from a dream.

'Of course it was? Who else do you think?'

And where had Jan been in his imagination? Who was the child he was carrying in his arms? Where were they going? And which country was he travelling through?

Jan wiped his hand across his brow and looked embarrassed. Then he answered Kattrinna: 'I thought they were King Herod of Judea and his wife Herodias!'

Scarlet Fever

When the little girl at Skrolycka was about three years old she fell ill with what must have been scarlet fever since her whole body was red and when you touched her she felt as if she was on fire. She wouldn't eat anything, nor could she sleep – she just lay there delirious. Jan couldn't bring himself to go out while she was ill, so he just stayed in the cottage day after day. It looked as if Farmer Erik's rye was not going to be threshed that year.

Kattrinna was the one looking after the girl, replacing the covers every time she threw them off and giving her sips of diluted blueberry juice the farmer's wife had let her have. When the little girl was healthy it was usually Jan who looked after her, but the moment she fell ill he was afraid to go near her. He was worried he wouldn't be able to handle her gently enough and might hurt her.

But he would not leave the cottage and just sat in the corner by the stove, gazing across at the small sick child.

She lay in her own bed with just a couple of straw pillows under her and no sheets. Lying on coarse linen covers must have felt hard and rough to a delicate little body made sensitive by swellings and sores.

What was really strange was that every time Jan saw her tossing and turning on the bed what came into his mind was his Sunday shirt, the very finest thing he owned in this world.

He only had the one and it was made of fine, gleaming white linen with a stiff front. It was so well-made it would have been quite good enough for the laird of Duvnäs and Jan treated it with the greatest respect. All the other clothes he wore were as coarse as the covers on the little girl's bed.

But it wasn't very sensible to think of the shirt. Kattrinna would never, not under any circumstances, agree to him destroying it, as it had been a wedding gift from her to him.

Kattrinna herself was doing everything she could. She borrowed the farmer's horse, wrapped the girl in shawls and blankets and took her to the doctor. That was well done on Kattrinna's part, though Jan couldn't see that it had done any good. The big bottle of drops she brought home from the chemist's was of no help, nor were the rest of the doctor's prescriptions.

It could be that the only way of holding on to a gift as precious as the little girl was to be prepared to sacrifice the very best thing he owned. But it wasn't easy to get someone like Kattrinna to understand that.

An old woman called Finn-Karin came to the cottage one day while the girl was ill. Like all those of the Finnish race, she knew ways to cure sick animals and she wasn't short of spells to banish sties and boils and whitlows, but people were reluctant to turn to her for other ailments. It didn't seem right to ask a witch for help with anything more than minor ills.

As soon as she entered the cottage she saw there was a sick child and Kattrinna told her the girl had scarlet fever, but they didn't ask the old woman for advice.

It was quite obvious to her, however, that the parents were deeply worried, and after Kattrinna had treated her to coffee and Jan given her some rolling tobacco, she said without prompting:

'It's beyond my powers to cure this illness. But this much I can tell you – you can discover whether the outcome will be life or death. Stay awake until midnight tonight and then put the tips of your left forefinger and your left little finger together so that they form an eye. Look at the little girl through that eye and see who is lying beside her in the bed. That will tell you what you can expect!'

Since it's always best to stay on the right side of people of that sort Kattrinna thanked her profusely, though not for one moment did she intend doing what the woman suggested.

Nor did Jan attach any importance to the woman's advice.

The only thing on his mind was the shirt. Knowing what Kattrinna would think, did he dare use it? It was quite out of the question to ask her to tear up the bridal gift she had given him. And he knew perfectly well the shirt couldn't make their little girl better, and if she were to die anyway, the shirt would have gone to waste.

Night fell and Kattrinna went to bed at her usual time, but Jan couldn't settle to sleep and stayed sitting up in the corner as he usually did. He watched Klara Goldie lying there in pain and discomfort. What she was lying on was so coarse and rough and he thought how sweet it would be to make her a bed that was cool and smooth and fine.

His shirt, newly washed and unworn, lay in the clothes chest. It pained him to know it was there, but he felt it wouldn't be fair to Kattrinna to use her gift as a sheet for the little girl.

Nevertheless, as the clock approached midnight and Kattrinna was sound asleep, something made him go over to the chest and take out the shirt. First he tore off the stiff front and then he ripped the shirt into two pieces. He slid one of them under Klara's small body and the other over her, between her and the thick, warm covers.

Then he went back to his corner and kept watch on her as before. He hadn't been there long before the clock struck twelve. Almost without thinking about what he was doing he made a circle with the fingers of his left hand, held them up in front of his eyes and looked towards the bed.

And behold! There, sitting on the edge of the bed, was a small, naked angel of the Lord, his skin scratched and raw from the coarse bedclothes, and it was obvious he had been on the point of leaving. But now he turned back, felt the fine shirt, stroked the soft linen with both hands and, without further ado, swung his legs back into the bed and lay down to watch over the child.

At the same time something black and foul was creeping up one of the bedposts, and when it saw that the angel of the Lord was about to leave it raised its head over the end of the bed with a leer of joy at the chance to creep into the bed and take his place.

But when it saw the angel of the Lord remain on guard, its limbs writhed and twisted and turned as if it was suffering all the agonising torments of the abyss as it slid back down to the floor.

The following day the child began to recover. Kattrinna was so happy to see the illness receding that she didn't have the heart to say anything about the destruction of the bridegroom's shirt, though we can be quite sure she thought she was married to a fool.

The Visit to the Farm

One Sunday afternoon when the little girl at Skrolycka was five years old, Jan Andersson took her by the hand and they walked together up into the forest.

They walked past the group of shady birch trees where they usually sat down. They walked past the patch where wild strawberries grew, and they even walked past the winding little burn, Tvättbäcken, without stopping.

They walked hand in hand, silently and earnestly, as if to show there was something very special about their errand.

They disappeared eastwards into the deepest part of the forest, but they didn't stop there either. Eventually they emerged on the wooded hillside above the village of Lobyn.

From there they went down to the crossroads where the highway and the village road met and now, at last, it must surely be obvious where they were heading.

But they didn't turn into Nästa Farm, nor into Nysta, and they didn't as much as look in the direction of Där Fram or På Valln.

They continued farther into the village and it was almost impossible to guess where they were actually going. Was it possible they were going to pay a visit to Björn Hindriksson in Lobyn? Surely not?

It was a fact, however, that Björn Hindriksson's wife was the half-sister of Jan's mother, so Jan was actually related to the richest people in the parish and had the right to call Björn Hindriksson and his wife uncle and aunt. Up until now Jan had never wanted to make anything of the relationship, and he had scarcely mentioned his elevated family connections

41

even to Kattrinna. He always avoided Björn Hindriksson and
didn't even go over and say hello or shake hands when people
were chatting outside church.

But now that Jan had such a remarkable little daughter, he
was no longer just a poor day labourer – now he had a treasure
to exhibit, a flower to show off. Now he was rich with the rich
and mighty with the mighty. So now, for the first time in his
life, he was walking straight up to Björn Hindriksson's house
to call upon his grand relations.

*

Their visit to the farm was not a long one. Less than an hour
later Jan and the little girl were walking back across the yard
to the gate.

But having got that far, Jan stopped and looked back as if he
wanted to return to the house.

He had no reason to regret their visit. They had been
well received in every way. Björn Hindriksson's wife had
immediately taken the girl over to a blue, painted cupboard
which stood in the middle of one of the long walls and given
her a rusk and a lump of sugar. And Björn Hindriksson himself
had asked how old she was and what she was called. Then he
had opened the big leather purse he carried in his trouser
pocket and given her a shining six öre silver coin.

Jan had been treated to coffee and his half-aunt asked
about Kattrinna and wondered whether they had a cow or a
pig, whether the cottage was cold in winter and whether his
day rate from Farmer Erik was enough for him to live on
without falling into debt.

No, Jan had no worries about how the visit itself had gone.
After he had talked to Björn Hindriksson and his wife for a
while, they had said – quite properly – that they were invited
to a party that afternoon and would have to leave in half an
hour. Jan – of course – understood that they needed time to
get ready and he stood up and bade them farewell.

Then his half-aunt had hurried over to her larder and taken
out some butter and bacon, filled a small bag with oats and a

second one with flour, wrapped them all in a bundle and given them to Jan to take with him. It was just a little something for him to take to Kattrinna, she said, who deserved some reward for having stayed at home keeping an eye on the house.

It was this bundle that Jan was now contemplating.

He recognised that it contained all kinds of good and fine things, the sort of things they longed for at every meal back at Skrolycka, but somehow he felt it was unfair to the little girl to accept it.

He had not visited Björn Hindriksson and his wife as a beggar but as a family visitor and he didn't want them to misunderstand that.

This thought had come to him while he was still in the house, but the respect he felt for Hindriksson and his wife was such that he hadn't dared do other than accept the bundle.

He walked back from the gate and placed the bundle by the corner of the stable, past which the people of the house walked all the time and so could not fail to see it.

It hurt to leave it behind, but his little girl was not a beggar child. No one was to be allowed to think that she and her father went round begging.

The School Examination

One spring day when the little girl was six years old Jan from Skrolycka went to Östanby School to listen to the school examination.

It was the first school building the parish had ever had and everyone thought how wonderful it was. Before that, Cantor Svartling and his pupils had no choice but to move from farm to farm.

Up until 1860 when the new schoolhouse was finished, he had been forced to change schoolroom every fortnight, and quite often he and his small pupils found themselves sharing a room in which the woman of the house was cooking and the man doing carpentry at his workbench, or where the old people were confined to bed all day and the hencoops were under the long bench.

In spite of this the teaching seemed to go well, for Cantor Svartling was a man who could command respect whatever the circumstances. But it must have been a treat for him to work in a room that was only used as a schoolroom. The walls would no longer be covered with foldaway bed cupboards and shelves for pots and pans and tools. No one would set up a loom in the window where the light was best, and there wouldn't be women neighbours dropping in for coffee and a chat during school hours.

Now, at last, he could decorate the walls with illustrations of Bible history, with animal pictures and portraits of the Kings of Sweden. The children had proper little desks and low benches rather than having to perch awkwardly around high gate-legged tables with their noses sometimes barely reaching the level of the tabletop. And Cantor Svartling had a desk of his own with shelves and pigeonholes in which there was space for the class registers. Now he had somewhere to sit with an air of authority for hours on end. It was very different from the past when all too often he had done his teaching while sitting on the hearth with a roaring fire at his back and all the children cross-legged on the floor in front of him. The blackboard now had its proper place and there were hooks for maps and charts so that they no longer had to be hung on cupboard doors and settles as had been done in the past.

He had somewhere to keep the quill pens and now had a chance to teach the children to draw straight lines and curves so that the whole parish would eventually end up with handwriting as beautiful as his. And he was able to teach the children all to stand up at the same time and to leave the room in good order like soldiers. There was no end to the improvements that could be introduced once the schoolhouse was ready.

Happy as everyone was with the new schoolhouse, there was nevertheless a sense in which parents felt there was a distance between themselves and their children once the children began attending it. It was as if something new and rather grand had been introduced to which the adults did not have access. But it was, of course, very unfair to look at it that way: they ought to be pleased that their children could enjoy the good things they had not been able to have.

The day that Jan from Skrolycka went to the school for the examination, he and little Klara Goldie, being the best of friends, walked the whole way hand in hand as they always did. But as they approached the schoolhouse and Klara saw the children gathered outside she withdrew her hand from his and moved over to the other side of the road. The moment they arrived she deserted him completely and went over and joined a group of children.

During the examination Jan from Skrolycka sat on a chair close to the teacher's desk, among the gentry and members of the school board. He'd had to take that particular seat otherwise he would only have seen the back of Klara's neck since she was seated on the very front bench to the right of the teacher's desk, along with the smallest children. In the past he would never have taken such an prominent position, but as the father of a little girl as special as Klara there was no need for him to feel inferior to anyone.

It was impossible for Klara not to see her father from where she was sitting, but she did not look his way once. It was as if he didn't exist for her.

But her eyes were fixed on the schoolmaster. He was in the process of testing the big children, whose place was to the left of his desk. They had to read and to point out countries and cities on the map and do sums on the blackboard. He barely had time to look over to the small children on his right. So it would have been no trouble for Klara to glance over to her father, but she didn't as much as turn her head in his direction.

It was some small comfort, of course, that all the children were behaving in the same manner. They sat with their bright little eyes fixed on the schoolmaster. And whenever he said something witty, the wee wretches would nudge one another, laugh and pretend to understand.

There can be no doubt that the parents were surprised to see their children behaving in such an exemplary way as they did during the examination. But Cantor Svartling was a remarkable man and there was little he could not get them to do.

For his part, Jan from Skrolycka began to feel both embarrassed and anxious. He no longer knew whether it was his own little girl sitting there or someone else's child. He began to ease his way out from his seat among the school board and move towards the door.

Eventually the testing of the big children came to an end and it was the turn of the small ones, those who had only just learnt to read. They had not yet acquired any great store of knowledge, but they nevertheless had to answer some questions. And they also had to show that they knew something of the story of Creation.

The first question put to them was 'Who created the world?' They had no difficulty with that, but then – very unfortunately – the teacher asked whether they knew any other name for God.

That was too much for these little beginners. They blushed, they furrowed their brows, but they could not think of an answer to such a testing question.

Hands shot up over on the big children's benches and there were sounds of whispering and sniggering. The eight small novices, however, just pursed their lips and couldn't say a word. Not Klara, nor a single one of the others.

'There is a prayer we say every day,' the teacher said. 'What do we call God then?'

Suddenly it came to Klara! She realised the teacher wanted them to answer that they often called God 'Father', and so she put up her hand.

'What is it we call God, then, Klara?' the schoolteacher said.

Klara stood up with her cheeks hot and red and the little stub of a plait at the back of her neck sticking straight out.

'We call him Jan!' she answered in a loud and clear voice.

A quiet snigger immediately ran through the whole schoolhouse. Gentry and members of the school board and parents and pupils could not keep their faces straight, and even the teacher looked amused.

Klara blushed and tears came to her eyes, but the teacher immediately rapped his pointer on the floor and called: 'Quiet!' Then he gave them a few words of explanation.

'What Klara meant was *father*, of course,' he said. 'And she said Jan instead because that's the name of her own father. Nor is there any need for us to wonder why the girl said what she said, because I don't know of any child in the school who has such a good father as she has. I have seen him waiting for her outside the schoolhouse in rain and in storm, and I've seen him carrying her to school when we've had blizzards and the roads are covered with snow. Little wonder, then, that she says Jan when she has to name the best thing she knows.'

The schoolteacher patted the girl on the head and all the people laughed and were moved at the same time.

Klara took her seat and looked down and didn't know what to do with herself, but Jan from Skrolycka was as happy as a king, because he suddenly realised that the little girl was still his and no one else's.

The Competition

There was something remarkable about the little girl from Skrolycka and her father. They looked as though they had been cut from the same piece of cloth and they were able to read one another's thoughts.

The schoolmaster in Svartsjö was an old soldier. He did his teaching in a distant part of the parish and, unlike the cantor, he didn't have a schoolhouse, but all of his children absolutely adored him. They didn't know they were attending school when they went to him, they thought they were just coming together to play.

The two schoolmasters were the very best of friends, but every so often the younger of the two would try to make the older man keep up with the times by introducing him, for instance, to the phonetic method or to other innovations. For the most part, the old fellow took these things in his stride, but for some reason there was one occasion on which he lost his temper.

'Having that new schoolhouse has really gone to your head, Svartling,' he said. 'But let me tell you something: we might have to do our work in farmhouses, but my children can read just as well as yours.'

'I know that, of course,' the cantor said, 'and I've never said otherwise. I simply mean that if there is something that makes it easier for the children to learn ...'

'And ...?' the older man said.

The cantor could tell from the tone of voice that he'd hurt him and so he tried to retreat.

'Anyway, you already make it so easy for your children that they never complain about their school work.'

'I make it too easy for them, is that it? I don't actually teach them anything, is that it?' the old man said, banging his fist on the table.

'What on earth's got into you today, Tyberg?' the cantor said. 'You're getting steamed up about everything I say.'

'Because you keep insinuating things all the time!'

People joined them at that point and by the time they parted the two schoolmasters had settled their differences and were good friends again. But once old Tyberg was alone on his way home, the cantor's words came back to him and he became almost angrier than he'd been before. 'What led that young whippersnapper to say that I'd be able to teach my children more than I do if I kept up to date?' he thought. 'I suppose he thinks I'm too old, though he wouldn't say it in so many words.'

He found it impossible to set his annoyance aside and when he arrived home he gave his wife a full account of everything.

'You mustn't let what the cantor says upset you,' she said. 'The young may be bright but the old are right is what I say. You are good teachers, both you and the cantor.'

'Yes, but it's not much help when you say it,' her husband answered. 'Other people will still think what they think.'

He spent the next couple of days looking so gloomy that his wife became really cross with him.

'Can't you show them how wrong they are?' she said.

'Show them what? What do you mean?'

'I mean, that if you know your pupils are as good as the cantor's ...'

'Of course I know they are.'

'Well then, you should ask for your pupils to be tested at the same time.'

The old fellow pretended not to pay any attention to what she had said but the thought struck home. A few days later the cantor received a letter in which the older teacher suggested that the children of the two schools should test their abilities against one another.

The cantor had nothing against the idea, but he wanted the competition to take place during the Christmas break, because then they could treat it as recreation for the children and he wouldn't have to ask permission from the school board.

'This is a really good idea, this is,' the cantor thought. 'I won't be needing to get them to redo their homework exercises this term.'

And he was right. The way the pupils in the two schools worked and swotted was little short of amazing.

The great competition was to take place on Boxing Day. The schoolroom was decorated with Christmas trees in which all the candles left over from the early church service on Christmas Day were shining. There were so many apples that there would easily be enough for every child to have two, and there was a rumour going round that parents and guardians who came to listen to the children were to be offered coffee.

But it was the grand competition itself that was the high point. On one side of the schoolroom sat Tyberg's children and on the other side the cantor's. Now it was up to the pupils to defend their teachers' reputations. Schoolmaster Tyberg was to examine the cantor's children and the cantor would examine Tyberg's children. If a question or a sum came up that one school could not manage, it would be passed over to the other school, and all the answers would then be totted up to decide which school performed best.

The cantor was the first to go and he made a cautious start, but once he realised how knowledgeable the children were he pushed them harder and harder. It was splendid to listen to Tyberg's children: they were absolutely rock-solid and did not let a single question pass to the other side.

Then it was Tyberg's turn to test the cantor's pupils.

The old man was no longer in a bad mood and since his own pupils had already shown that they knew their stuff he felt like a bit of devilment. At first he asked the cantor's children proper questions, but he didn't stay serious for long and very soon he was being as jolly and amusing as he was in his own school.

'Right, now I know you have all read much more than we have read over here in the back of beyond,' he said. 'You've done nature study and stuff like that. But I wonder if any of you can tell me what the rocks are like in the Motala River.'

Not one of the cantor's pupils put a hand up, but over on Tyberg's side of the room up went hand after hand!

Sitting among the cantor's pupils was Olof Olsson, a boy who knew he had the best brain in the parish, and there was also August Där Nol, son of a good farming family – but neither of them had a word to say. Sitting there, too, was Karin Svens, the bright lass from the soldier's croft – she had never missed a single day of school – but all she could do, just like the rest of them, was to sit there thinking how odd it was that the cantor hadn't taught them what was special about the rocks in the Motala River.

And there sat Klara Fina Goldenborg from Skrolycka, a girl who had been named after the sun, in spite of which her mind was as dark as everyone else's.

Schoolmaster Tyberg was standing there with a serious look on his face while the cantor, deeply concerned, just stared down at the floor.

'I suppose there's nothing for it, then – I shall have to pass this question to the other side,' the schoolmaster said. 'Who would have thought that not one of you keen lads and lasses can give me an answer to such a simple question!'

At the very last minute Klara from Skrolycka turned round and, as she usually did when she didn't know what else to do, looked over at her father Jan. Jan was so far away from Klara that he couldn't whisper in her ear, but the moment she caught her father's eye she knew what she had to say.

She was so eager she didn't just put her hand up, she stood up straight.

All of her schoolmates turned in her direction, and the cantor looked happy that the question was not about to be taken away from his pupils.

'They are all wet!' she called out without waiting to be asked, because there was no time left to waste.

The next moment she thought she had given such a stupid answer that she had ruined everything for all of them. She sank back down on the bench and almost slid under the desk so that no one could see her.

'Well now, my girl, that is the correct answer!' the schoolmaster said. 'It was just as well that someone in the cantor's class could answer the question because, for all your cockiness, you were about to lose the game.'

The children on both sides, some of the grown-ups too, burst out laughing. And some of the children were laughing so much they had to stand up while others had to put their heads down on the desk. Discipline went out of the window.

'Now then, I think we'll move the desks out of the way and take a turn around the Christmas tree,' old Tyberg said.

And never had so much fun been had in the schoolhouse before – nor since for that matter.

The Catch of Fish

I t was obviously impossible for anyone to love the little girl
at Skrolycka as much as her father did, but we can also say
for sure that she had a really good friend in Ola, the old net
maker.

The friendship between them began one spring when Klara
started setting fixed lines for the small brown trout that lived
in the Tvättbäcken burn. Her luck was better than might have
been expected and on her very first day she came home with a
couple of little fish.

She was proud of herself, which is understandable, and
even her mother praised her for being able to bring home food
when she was no more than eight years old. To encourage her,
Kattrinna let her clean and fry the fish and Jan ate some of it
and said he had never tasted a fish like it. That was no more
than the plain truth since the fish was so bony, dry and smoky
that even the little girl could scarcely get a mouthful down.

But she kept at her fishing for all that. Every morning she
rose at the same time as Jan himself. Over her arm she would
hang a basket in which to carry her fish home and she took
a small tin box of worms to rebait the hooks that had been
nibbled clean. Thus equipped she would walk up along the
Tvättbäcken as it came dancing down from the high ground
over steep falls and long cataracts between which there were
dark, still pools and clear stretches where the water flowed
gently and transparently over sand and smooth rocks.

But, strange as it may seem, her successful fishing lasted no
longer than the first week. After that the worms disappeared
from most of the hooks without any fish being hooked. She
moved her tackle from cataract to still water and from still

water to steep falls and she replaced her hooks, but there was no improvement.

She asked the boys at Börje's place and over at Erik's whether they were rising early in the morning and taking her fish. They scarcely bothered to answer, for no boys were going to stoop to fishing the Tvättbäcken when they had the whole of Lake Duvsjön to fish in. Running around fishing in forest streams was all right for little girls who weren't allowed down by the lake.

However brazenly the boys denied it, she wasn't sure she really believed them. There had to be someone who was taking the fish from her hooks – after all, the hooks she was setting out in the Tvättbäcken were real hooks, not just bent pins.

Eventually, in order to discover the truth, she rose one morning earlier than Jan and Kattrinna and hurried to the burn. As she approached it she slowed down and walked on tiptoe, taking care not to trip over stones or rustle the bushes.

And what did she find? When she reached the edge of the burn she froze from head to toe. She saw she had been right: the fish thief was standing just where she had set out her lines the morning before and he was checking them.

It was a grown man, though, not one of the boys she had thought it would be. He was standing bent over the water and was pulling in a fish at that very moment. She could see how it glistened as he took it off the hook.

Klara was no more than eight years old but nothing frightened her and she ran forward to catch the thief red-handed.

'So you're the one who's been taking my fish!' she said. 'It's a good thing I caught you this time – now there'll be an end to this thieving!'

At this point the man raised his head and Klara saw his face. It was the old net maker who lived in one of the nearby cottages.

'I know that this is your tackle, all this,' he said quite calmly, without becoming angry or heated as people usually do when they are caught doing something wrong.

'What makes you think you can take what doesn't belong to

you?' the little girl said.

The man gave her a look she would never forget. She felt she was gazing into two open, empty chasms in which there lay two half-dead eyes that were beyond both sorrow and joy.

'It's like this – I know you get everything you need from your parents and that you fish for pleasure. But in my home we are close to dying of starvation.'

The little girl's face blushed bright red. Without knowing why, she was now the one who felt ashamed.

The net maker did not say anything else. He picked up his cap, which had fallen off when he bent over the hooks, and departed.

Nor did Klara say anything. Two fish were flapping on the bank, but she did not pick them up and, after standing there watching them for a while, she kicked them back into the water.

For the rest of that day the little girl felt displeased with herself, although she could not understand why. After all, she wasn't the one who had been in the wrong.

She could not get the old net maker out of her mind. People said there had been a time when he was rich. He was said to have owned seven farms, each of them worth as much as Erik's farm at Falla. But somehow, in some strange way, he had lost everything and was now as poor as a church mouse.

The following morning, in spite of everything, she went back to the Tvättbäcken and inspected her hooks. This time no one had interfered with them and she found fish on every hook. She unhooked the fish and put them in her basket, but she did not make her way home. Instead, she went straight to the net maker's place.

When Klara arrived carrying her basket, the old man was chopping wood outside his cottage. She stopped at the stile and watched him before climbing over. His clothes were poor and ragged. She had never seen her own father look like that.

She'd heard people say that there were well-to-do folk who had offered to take him in until his dying day, but he'd moved here instead, to Askedalarna, to live with his daughter-in-law and help her as best he could. She had many small children and her husband had left her long before and was thought to be dead.

'Lots of fish on the hooks today!' the little girl shouted from the stile.

'There were, were there?' the net maker said. 'That's really good then.'

'I'm happy to give you all the fish I catch, as long as I can do the fishing myself,' the little girl said.

She walked over to him and emptied her basket at his feet. Then she waited for the net maker to be pleased and praise her as her father Jan usually did. Everything she said and did made Jan happy.

But the net maker reacted in the same calm way as he always did.

'You keep what belongs to you!' he said. 'We are so used to going hungry here that we can easily do without a couple of little fish.'

There was something quite strange about this poor old man. But Klara simply would not give up until she had made him like her.

'You can bait the hooks and take the fish – the whole lot,' was her next offer.

'No, I don't want to take that pleasure away from you,' the old man said.

But Klara just stood there. She did not want to leave until she had found a way of satisfying him.

'Do you want me to come here and fetch you every morning so that we can check the hooks together? And each of us gets half of the fish?'

The old man stopped chopping. He looked at her with those strange, careworn eyes of his and the shadow of a smile crossed his face.

'Now you've hooked me at last,' he said. 'I won't say no to that suggestion.'

Agrippa

She really was truly remarkable, this little girl. At no more than ten years of age she showed herself capable of coping with a man like Agrippa Prästberg.

We only have to remember what he looked like to understand why almost everyone took care not to fall out with him. His eyes, beneath bushy eyebrows, were yellow and red-rimmed; his nose was horribly crooked; a great tousled beard bristled around his mouth; his brow was deeply furrowed and his tall gangly frame was crowned by a tattered soldier's cap. No wonder, then, that most people were afraid to cross him.

One day the little girl was sitting on her own on the smooth stone slab by the cottage door eating a slice of bread and butter for supper when she caught sight of a tall man coming up the road. It didn't take her long to realise it was Agrippa Prästberg.

But she didn't lose her head, far from it. The first thing she did was break her bread in half and put one piece on top of the other so it wouldn't smear her dress when she tucked it under her apron.

After that she remained sitting where she was. She didn't run away and she didn't try to barricade the cottage – she knew there was no point in doing that with a man like Agrippa. What she did, however, was to pick up the sock Kattrina had been knitting and left lying on the slab when she went to take Jan's supper to his work a short time before.

The needles clicked as Klara began knitting and she sat there trying to look really calm and unconcerned, although she was surreptitiously keeping one eye on the gate. No, she wasn't mistaken. He was lifting the hook and was intending to come in.

She moved a little farther up the slab and spread out her skirts, for she knew that it was now up to her to take care of their home.

Klara, of course, knew enough about Agrippa to know that he wasn't the sort to steal things, nor was he given to violence as long as no one called him 'Grippa' or offered him a slice of bread. Nor did he spend very long at each of the places he visited unless the inhabitants were unlucky enough to have a Mora clock in the house.

He was in the habit of going round the whole district mending clocks, and if he came to a cottage which possessed one of those tall, old grandfather clocks he wasn't satisfied until they allowed him to take out the clockwork to check whether there was anything wrong with it. And there always was something wrong, which meant he had no choice but to take the whole clock to pieces. The likelihood then was that it would take him a good few days to put it all back together again, and during that time he had to be housed and fed.

Worse still, however, was the fact that once Prästberg got his hands on a clock, it would never run as well as it had before. After that there was no choice but to let Prästberg come and attend to the clock at least once a year, otherwise it would stop. There's no doubt the old fellow tried do his work conscientiously and honestly but, however that may be, the clocks were ruined.

Which is why it was best to keep him away from the family clock, as Klara knew only too well. But now she couldn't see any way of saving their Mora clock, which was ticking away in the cottage. Prästberg knew it was there and he'd been trying to get at it for some time, but on the other occasions when he'd turned up, Kattrinna had been at home to stop him.

When the old fellow reached the cottage he came to a halt right in front of the little girl, struck his staff hard against the ground and rattled off:

'Here comes Johan Utter Agrippa Prästberg, Drummer to His Majesty and to the Crown. He has faced both bullets and powder and neither angels nor devils frighten him! Is there anyone at home?'

There was no need for Klara to answer, for he strode straight past her into the cottage and made for the Mora clock.

The girl ran after him, trying to tell him what good time the clock was keeping. It was neither fast nor slow and it certainly didn't need mending.

'How can a clock possibly keep good time if Johan Utter Agrippa Prästberg hasn't seen to it?' he said.

He was so tall that he was able to open the clock case without climbing on a chair and in no time at all he had removed the dial and the mechanism and put them on the table. Klara clenched her fists under her apron and tears came to her eyes, but there was nothing she could do to stop him.

Prästberg was in a great hurry to find something wrong with the clock before Jan and Kattrinna could come home and tell him it did not need mending. He was carrying a small bundle of tools and tins of grease, which he quickly opened, but he was in such a hurry that some of the things fell to the floor.

He ordered Klara to pick everything up, and anyone who knows Agrippa Prästberg will understand that she didn't dare do other than obey. She went down on the floor and passed him a small saw and a screwdriver.

'Anything else down there?' the old man roared. 'You can think yourself lucky to have the chance to serve the Drummer to his Royal Majesty and the Crown, you miserable little cottar's child!'

'Not as far as I can see,' the girl answered, more dejected and unhappy than she had ever been. After all, she was supposed to be looking after the cottage for her mother and father and now this was happening.

'What about my glasses?' Prästberg asked. 'They must have fallen down there too.'

'No,' the girl said. 'No glasses down here.'

And all of a sudden she saw a spark of hope. He wouldn't be able to do anything to the clock without them, would he? What if he couldn't find his glasses?

She caught sight of his spectacle case, which was lying

behind the leg of the table.

The old man rummaged around through all the old cogs and springs he had in his bundle of tools. With any luck, there was a chance that he wouldn't find his glasses.

'I suppose there's nothing for it,' he said. 'I'll have to come down and look myself. Up you get, you little wretch!'

Klara's hand shot out like lightning, snatched the spectacle case and tucked it under her apron.

'Up with you!' the old man grunted. 'I don't know whether to believe you. What's that you've got under your apron? Out with it! Do as I say now!'

Klara immediately held out one of her hands – she had been keeping the other one hidden under her apron the whole time. But now she had to show him that one too, and that meant showing him her sandwich.

'Ugh! It's a sandwich,' Agrippa Prästberg said, recoiling as if the little girl was holding out an adder.

'I was eating it outside when you came and I hid it because I know you don't like butter.'

Agrippa went down on the floor and searched, but he searched in vain.

'You must have left them behind where you were last,' Klara said.

He'd been thinking the same thing himself, though he didn't really want to believe it.

In any case, without his glasses there was nothing he could do about the clock. He had no choice but to bundle up his tools and put the works back in the clock. While his back was turned the little girl slipped the spectacle case into his bundle.

And that's where he found it after returning to Lövdala Manor, the last place he had worked. He was just about to enquire about his spectacles and when he opened his bundle to show they weren't there, the spectacle case was the first thing he saw.

The next time he saw Jan and Kattrinna outside the church he went over to them and spoke:

'That little girl of yours,' he said, 'that clever little girl of yours, she'll bring you joy, that one.'

Forbidden Fruit

There were, in fact, many people who told Jan from Skrolycka that his little girl would bring him joy when she grew up. People simply did not seem to understand that she already made him happy every hour of every day that God gave him. There was only one occasion in all the time she was growing up when she gave him cause to be both angry and ashamed.

On the seventeenth of August in the summer of the year she was eleven years old she and Jan were walking over the hill to Lövdala. That day was the birthday of Lieutenant Liljekrona, the estate owner.

The seventeenth of August was a day of such joy that everyone in Svartsjö and Bro looked forward to it for the whole year. The joy was felt not only by the gentlefolk who would be taking part in the celebrations, but also by large numbers of children and young people from the countryside all round who came to Lövdala to see the gentry dressed in their finery and to listen to the singing and dance music.

But there was also something else that made a trip to Lövdala on the seventeenth of August particularly attractive to the young: at that time of year the garden there was full of tasty things. They had, of course, been brought up to be honest in almost every way, but when it came to what was hanging on bushes and trees under open skies, they felt they could pick as much as they wanted. As long as they were careful not to be caught.

When Jan and Klara entered the garden he noticed at once how wide her eyes grew at the sight of all the fine apple trees weighed down with plump, green, unripe fruit. And he was unlikely to have denied her a bite if he hadn't noticed that Söderlind, the grieve, and a couple of other people from the estate were keeping a look-out to prevent any damage being done.

Jan took Klara to the courtyard where there wasn't anything to tempt her, but he must have known that her mind was still back among the gooseberry bushes and apple trees, for she paid no attention to the young and elegantly dressed gentlefolk nor to the pretty flower beds. He couldn't get her to listen to the fine speeches in honour of Lieutenant Liljekrona that were given by the dean of Bro and Boraeus, the engineer from Borg. She didn't even want to listen to the congratulatory verses which Cantor Svartling had composed.

From inside the house the sounds of Anders Öster's clarinet could be heard and the dance music he was playing was so jolly that people found it difficult to keep their feet still. But the little girl was only interested in finding an excuse to go back to the garden.

Jan hung doggedly on to her hand the whole time, not letting go whatever excuse she came up with. And he was successful until evening came.

As darkness fell coloured lanterns were hung in the trees and set out on the ground among the flowers and up among the dense creepers that climbed the walls of the house. It was so beautiful that Jan, who had never seen anything like it before, grew light-headed and unsure whether he was still on this earth. But he still kept a firm hold of that little hand.

Once the lanterns were lit, the man who kept the store down by the church, together with his brother and Anders Öster and his nephew, began singing, and as they sang Jan felt a strange, powerful current of joy flowing through the air and washing away all troubles and cares. It came so quietly and sweetly in the warmth of the night that Jan found it irresistible. It affected everyone in the same way and they all felt happy to be alive and to have such a beautiful world to live in.

'You can tell it's the seventeenth of August, can't you,' the people around him whispered.

'This must be what it was like for those who dwelt in Paradise,' a young man said, with a look of great solemnity.

Jan felt exactly as they did, but he still had enough self-control not to let go of the child's hand.

After the singing, rockets were fired. The small fiery projectiles rose high in the deep-blue night sky before breaking into a shower of red, blue and yellow stars that made Jan feel humble and exalted at the same time. Then, for just one moment, he forgot Klara and by the time he came to his senses she had gone.

'Well,' Jan thought, 'there's nothing for it but to hope she has her usual good fortune and the grieve and his watchmen don't catch her.'

There was no point trying to find her in the darkness in that big garden. The best thing to do was to stay where he was and wait for her.

He didn't have long to wait. Another song was just coming to an end when Jan caught sight of Söderlind, the grieve, carrying Klara.

Lieutenant Liljekrona and a number of other gentlemen were standing at the top of the front steps listening to the song. The grieve came to a halt in front of him and put the little girl down on the step.

Klara didn't howl, nor did she make any attempt to run away. She had picked an apron full of apples and her only thought was to hang on to her apron so that none of the apples fell out.

'This child was up in one of the apple trees,' the grieve said. 'And you did say, sir, that if I nabbed anyone stealing your apples you'd be wanting a word with them yourself, sir.'

Lieutenant Liljekrona looked at the little girl and the little wrinkles around his eyes began to twitch. It was impossible to tell at that moment whether he was about to laugh or weep.

He had clearly been intending to give anyone caught stealing his apples a serious talking to, but when he saw the way the little girl was clutching her apron, his heart filled with sympathy for her instead. It was just that he couldn't think of a way of letting her keep the apples. If he let her go without further ado, it might lead to his whole garden being stripped bare.

'So you've been up in my apple trees, have you?' he said. 'You go to school, don't you, and you must have read about Adam and Eve, haven't you? So you surely know it's dangerous to steal apples?'

At that moment Jan stepped forward and stood beside Klara. He was really displeased with her for having spoilt the great joy he was feeling, but he had to stand shoulder to shoulder with her anyway.

'Don't do anything to the little girl, lieutenant,' he said. 'I was the one who gave her permission to climb the tree and take the apples.'

No sooner had he spoken than Klara gave her father an indignant look and broke her silence. 'That's not true,' she said. 'I was the one who wanted apples. Father's been holding on to my hand the whole evening to stop me taking them.'

This really pleased the lieutenant.

'You've done the right thing there, my girl,' he said. 'You were quite right not to let your father take the blame. You know that when Our Lord became angry with Adam and Eve it wasn't because they stole the apples but because they were so cowardly that they put the blame on each other. You can go now, and since you weren't afraid to tell the truth you can keep the apples.'

He turned to one of his sons.

'Give Jan a glass of arrack,' he said. 'We'll drink a toast with him because his lass gave a better answer than Eve did in the days of old. It would have been better for all of us if Klara had been in the Garden of Eden instead of Eve!'

II.

Lars Gunnarsson

One cold winter's day Erik at Falla and Jan from Skrolycka were up in the forest cutting timber.

They had sawn though a thick tree trunk and the tree was about to fall, so they moved to one side to be clear of the branches when the tree hit the ground.

'Watch yourself, master!' Jan said. 'I think it will come your way.'

There would have been plenty of time for Erik to jump out of the way while the spruce tree stood weighing up its options. But Erik had felled so many trees in his life that he thought he was a better judge than Jan and so he remained where he was. A moment later he was lying outstretched on the ground with the tree on top of him.

He didn't make a sound when he went down and the branches of the spruce covered him so completely that he was invisible. Jan stood there looking around, with no idea where his master had gone.

Then he heard the familiar old voice he had been obeying all his life, but now it was so weak he could hardly make out what it was saying.

'Jan, go and fetch help and a horse to get me home!'

'Shouldn't I help you out from under there first?' Jan asked. 'It must be painful lying there?'

'Do as I say, Jan!' Erik said. And Jan, knowing of old that his master was the sort who above all wanted to be obeyed, did as he was told without further objection.

So Jan ran back to Falla as fast as he was able, but it wasn't the nearest farm by any means and it took him quite a time to get there.

The first of the farm folk he encountered was Lars Gunnarsson. Lars was married to Erik's eldest daughter and was the man chosen to take over the farm when the old farmer passed away.

As soon as Lars Gunnarsson heard the news he told Jan to go into the house and tell the farmer's wife what had happened, and then to go and find the farm boy. Meanwhile Lars himself would run to the stable and harness one of the horses.

'We surely don't need to tell the women about the accident right away, do we?' Jan said. 'If they start crying and going on, it's bound to hold us up. We'd better hurry – Erik's voice sounded very weak under that tree.'

But ever since coming to the farm Lars Gunnarsson had been at pains to make people respect him, and once he had given a command he was no more likely to take it back than his father-in-law was.

'Go in and tell the mistress!' he said. 'Can't you see that they need to make a bed ready so there is somewhere to put him when we bring him home?'

So Jan had to go in to the farmer's wife and tell her what had happened and how, and although he did his best to hurry, it still took some time.

When Jan went back out to the yard he could hear Lars roaring and swearing in the stable. Lars was useless at handling animals and the horses kicked out the moment he approached. He hadn't managed to lead any of them out of the loose-box during the whole time Jan had been talking to the farmer's wife.

Jan knew that any attempt to help would not be welcome and he set off instead on the other errand, which was to find the farm boy. He thought it more than a little strange that it hadn't occurred to Lars to tell him to talk to Börje, who was threshing in the nearby barn, rather than go for the boy, who was thinning birch saplings in a copse some distance from the farmyard.

While Jan was going about these unnecessary errands, his ears could still hear the sound of that weak voice under the branches of the tree. It was no longer sounding so commanding now, it was begging and praying him to hurry.

'I'm coming, I'm coming,' Jan whispered back. But he had that feeling you get when you're trapped in a nightmare and can't move from the spot however hard you try.

At last Lars got the horse into the traces, but then the women came out and told him to take straw and covers with him. They were quite right, but it meant there was another delay before everything was ready.

Eventually they left the farm, Lars, Jan and the farm boy, but they had gone no farther than the edge of the forest before Lars stopped the horse.

'News of this kind puts your mind in a spin,' he said. 'I've only just realised that Börje was in the barn.'

'Yes,' Jan said. 'It would have been good to have him with us. He's twice as strong as any of us.'

So Lars ordered the boy to run back to the farm and fetch Börje, which meant another delay.

While Jan was sitting there on the sledge unable to do anything, he felt a great, empty, icy cold chasm opening within him, dark and dreadful to peer into. But at the same time he knew it wasn't a chasm, just the certainty they were going to be too late.

At last Börje and the boy came running up, panting breathlessly, and they all set off into the forest.

But they were still moving slowly, for the horse Lars had harnessed to the sledge was Brownie, who was old and stiff-legged. There was clearly more than a pinch of truth in what he'd said about his head being in a spin.

And it wasn't long before there was more evidence that his mind was in a muddle – he wanted them to turn off and take the wrong road. 'No,' Jan said. 'If we go that way we shall end up on Storsnipa Hill, but we want the forest above Lobyn.'

'I know that,' Lars said. 'But there is a side road farther up and it's better than this one.'

'What side road is that?' Jan asked. 'I've never seen one.'

'Just you wait and you'll see!' He wanted them to set off up the hill at once, but this time Börje supported Jan, and Lars had to give way. But the argument had wasted even more time and Jan could feel the black void spreading through his whole body. He felt his arms and hands becoming so numb and hollow that he couldn't move them.

'It makes no difference now,' he thought. 'We shall be too late. Erik won't be needing our help by the time we get there.'

The old horse struggled along the forest road as well as it could, but it didn't have the strength for a journey of this kind. It was poorly shod and time after time it stumbled. When the road ran uphill the men had to get down and walk, and when it was time to turn off into the trackless forest Brownie was more of a hindrance than a help.

They arrived at last and found Erik in a reasonable state. The tree hadn't crushed him or broken anything, but he had a deep wound where one of his thighs had been torn by a branch. It was nothing he couldn't recover from.

When Jan arrived for work the following morning he was told that Erik had a high temperature and was in severe pain. Lying so long on the ground had given him a chill, which turned into pneumonia. A fortnight after his accident he died.

The Red Dress

One summer Sunday when the young girl from Skrolycka was seventeen years old she was walking to church together with her parents. During the walk there she had been wearing a shawl, which she removed on arriving outside the church, allowing everyone to see that she was wearing a dress that no one in the parish had seen the like of.

One of the pedlars who travel the country with great packs on their backs had come to Askedalarna, and when he saw Klara in all the fresh splendour of her youth he had produced this cloth from his bag and tried to convince the girl's parents to buy it for her. It was red and its colour shifted almost as if it were silk.

The cloth was as expensive as it was beautiful and there was no chance that Jan and Kattrinna could afford to buy enough for a dress for the girl, although Jan, anyway, would have liked nothing better.

The strange thing was that after the pedlar had coaxed and cajoled them in vain, he became so intent on getting his own way that common sense deserted him. He told them he hadn't seen anyone in the district on whom the cloth would look as beautiful as on their daughter and his mind was set on her having it.

Then he measured out the length needed for a dress and gave it to Klara. He wasn't interested in payment, all he asked was to see her wearing the red dress the next time he came to Skrolycka.

The dress was made up by the best seamstress in the parish, a woman who did the sewing for the ladies at Lövdala. And when Klara put the dress on, the two of them together – Klara and the dress – were so pretty you'd be forgiven for thinking they had grown as naturally as the fruits on a beautiful dog rose bush in the wood.

On the Sunday that Klara was to wear the red dress to church, Jan and Kattrinna were so curious to hear what people would say that neither of them wanted to stay at home.

And, of course, everyone noticed the red dress, and having noticed it once, they turned to take another look. But when they looked the second time it was the young girl they were seeing, not just the dress she was wearing.

Some of them had already heard the story of the dress and others wanted to know how a poor lass from a croft could be so well-turned-out among all the people gathered outside the church. Jan and Kattrinna were pressed to tell the tale of the pedlar time and time again, and once people heard how it had come about, they no longer had any reason to feel annoyed. They were all happy that good fortune had paid a visit to a poor cottage away up in Askedalarna.

The sons of the yeoman farmers actually made no bones about saying that if this girl had been from the right sort of family she would have been betrothed to someone before she left the church.

And some of the farmers' daughters, even those in line of inheritance, admitted to themselves that they wouldn't hesitate to give a year's crops in exchange for a face so rosy and glowing with youth and health.

It just happened that the preacher in Svartsjö that Sunday was the dean of Bro rather than the usual minister. The dean was both stern and old-fashioned and any kind of extravagance in dress or in any other respect angered him.

When he saw the young girl in the red dress it seems that he feared it might be silk, so he sent the cantor to fetch the girl and her parents in order to have a word with them.

Even he had no difficulty in seeing that the girl and the dress were perfectly matched, but that did not make him any the less displeased.

'Listen to me now, my girl,' he said to Klara, putting his hand on her shoulder. 'There is nothing to prevent me hanging a gold cross around my neck and dressing like a bishop if that is what I want to do. But I don't do so, because I have no wish to appear grander than I am. And you should do likewise. You are the daughter of a poor cottar and should not be dressing like a mamsell of the manor.'

These were stern words and Klara was so dismayed she couldn't think of an answer. Kattrinna, however, hastened to tell him that the girl had been given the fabric as a present.

'That might well be the case,' the dean said. 'But you as parents should understand that if you allow your daughter to dress up like that once or twice, you will find it impossible to get her to wear the humble sort of clothes you can afford for her.'

Having made his point in words that could not be misunderstood he turned to leave. But while the dean was still in earshot, Jan had an answer ready.

'If this little girl were dressed as she should be,' he said, 'she would be as splendid as the sun, because she has been a sun and a joy for us ever since she was born.'

The dean came back and looked thoughtfully at all three of them. Both Jan and Kattrinna looked old and worn, but although their faces were wrinkled their eyes shone when they gazed at the glowing youth of the girl standing between them.

Then the dean must have said to himself that it would be a pity to upset the contentment of these old people, and he said in a mild voice: 'If it is true that you've brought light and joy to your poor parents, then you can wear your dress with honour. For a child that can bring happiness to its mother and father is the best thing our eyes can behold.'

The New Owner

When the Skrolycka folk arrived home from church on the Sunday the dean had said those beautiful words to Klara they found two men perched on the fence close to the gate.

One of them was Lars Gunnarsson, who had become master of the farm after the death of Erik, and the other was the assistant from a shop in Broby where Kattrinna usually bought her sugar and coffee.

They looked so casual, so out-of-place, sitting there that Jan found it hard to believe they had come to see him, so all he did was raise his cap and walk past them into the cottage without saying a word.

They remained where they were and Jan wished they would move somewhere else so he didn't have to look at them. He knew Lars Gunnarsson bore him ill will since the day of the accident in the forest. On more than one occasion he had heard him suggest that Jan was getting old and no longer merited his day's pay.

Kattrinna made dinner and the family soon finished eating, meanwhile Lars Gunnarsson and the shop assistant were still sitting out there on the fence, chatting away cheerfully. Jan thought they were perched there like a pair of hawks, enjoying themselves, biding their time and having fun at the expense of the songbirds that believed they could evade them.

Eventually, however, they climbed down from the fence, opened the gate and approached the cottage. So they did have business with Jan.

His premonition that they did not mean well was so strong that he looked around as if seeking a corner to hide in. But when his eyes fell on Klara, who was also looking out of the window, his courage returned.

What did he have to be afraid of when he had a daughter like her. She was clever and quick-witted and frightened of nothing, and fortune was always on her side, whatever she undertook. It wouldn't be easy for Lars Gunnarsson to get the better of her.

When Lars Gunnarsson and the shop assistant came in they behaved just as off-handedly as before. Lars said that having spent so long sitting on the fence looking at the pretty little cottage they eventually felt an urge to look inside.

They praised everything they saw and Lars expressed the opinion that Jan and Kattrinna ought to be grateful to Erik at Falla who, when all was said and done, was the one who had made it possible for the cottage to be built and for them to marry.

'And something else occurs to me,' he said immediately afterwards, turning away so that his eyes avoided both Jan and Kattrinna. 'I'm sure Erik would have had the forethought to give you papers proving that the ground the cottage occupies belongs to you?'

Neither Jan nor Kattrinna said a word. They realised immediately that Lars had come to the point he wanted to discuss with them. For a start, anyway, it might be best to let him give a clear explanation of what he had in mind.

'I've heard,' Lars said, 'that there are no papers, though I can't really believe things are quite that bad. If they are, however, it's possible that the whole cottage goes to whoever owns the ground.'

Jan still said nothing, but Kattrinna grew so angry that she could no longer stay silent.

'Erik at Falla Farm gave us the plot the cottage stands on,' she said, 'and no one has the right to take it away from us.'

The new owner assured them in a conciliatory voice that he had no intention of doing so. He just wanted everything to be in proper order. Now if Jan could give him a hundred riksdaler before the October market ...

'A hundred riksdaler!' Kattrinna exclaimed, her voice

almost rising to a shriek.

Lars did not say any more. He drew his head back and pursed his lips.

'You haven't said a word, Jan, you haven't!' Kattrinna said. 'Didn't you hear him, Jan? Lars wants to take a hundred riksdaler from us.'

'Jan probably won't find it easy to come up with a hundred riksdaler,' Lars Gunnarsson said. 'But I've every right to know what belongs to me, don't I?'

'And so you're going to steal our cottage, are you?' Kattrinna screamed.

'No, that's not what I'm going to do. The cottage is yours – it's just the land it stands on that I want!'

'Which means that the cottage has to move from your land,' Kattrinna said.

'It may not be worth your while going to the trouble of moving something you can't keep anyway.'

'I see,' Kattrinna said. 'So you do want to get your paws on it, after all.'

Lars Gunnarsson waved his hand dismissively. No, he did not want to confiscate the cottage. Heavens no! He had told them that, hadn't he? But the thing was that the shopkeeper in Broby had sent this shop assistant with some bills for which he was still awaiting payment.

The shop assistant took out the bills and Kattrinna pushed them across to Klara and asked her to work out what they added up to.

What was owed was no less than a hundred riksdaler, and Kattrinna's face went completely pale.

'I see you are intending to drive us from house and home,' she said.

'No, that's not the intention at all,' Lars answered. 'Not if you pay what you owe ...'

'You ought to think about your own parents,' Kattrinna said. 'They didn't have an easy life, did they, not until you became the son-in-law of a yeoman farmer.'

It was Kattrinna who had been doing all the talking whereas Jan had said nothing, he just sat there looking at

Klara, looking and waiting. It seemed so obvious to him that all this was happening on her account and she would have an opportunity to show what she was capable of.

'Take away a poor man's cottage and that's him finished,' Kattrinna wailed.

'I don't want to take the cottage,' Lars Gunnarsson defended himself. 'I just want the bills to be settled.'

But Kattrinna wasn't listening to him. 'As long as a poor man has a cottage he feels he is as good as everyone else. But a man without a home of his own doesn't even feel human.'

Jan thought that everything Kattrinna was saying was right. The cottage was built of scrap timber and it was cold in the winter. Small and cramped it might be, and it leaned over at an angle on uneven ground, but if they were to lose it ...? Well, they felt that would be the end.

Jan for his part could not believe for one moment that things could go so badly wrong. After all, Klara was sitting there and he could see the beginnings of a gleam in her eyes. She would soon have something to say. Or she would do something to drive these tormentors away.

'You can have time to reach a decision, of course,' the new owner said. 'But bear this in mind, either you move out by the first of October or the shopkeeper in Broby is paid in full. And I must have a hundred riksdaler for the plot!'

Kattrinna sat there wringing her work-worn old hands. She was so upset that she was talking to herself without worrying whether anyone else could hear her.

'How can I go to church, how can I show my face in public when I'm such a pauper I no longer have a cottage to call my own?'

Jan's mind was on other things. He was remembering the beautiful memories that went with the cottage. It was here that the midwife had handed him the baby. Over there by the door was where he had stood when the sun peeped out from the clouds and gave the girl her name. The cottage was part of him and Klara and Kattrinna. It could not be taken from them.

He saw how Klara was clenching one of her hands. Surely

she would soon come up with an idea to help them?

Lars Gunnarsson and the shop assistant stood up and went towards the door. They said goodbye as they departed, but none of the three left in the cottage responded.

As soon as they were gone, the girl tossed her head back proudly and stood up.

'If only you would let me to go out into the world!' she said.

Kattrinna stopped muttering and wringing her hands. The words had sparked a thin glimmer of hope.

'It can't be completely impossible to earn two hundred riksdaler by the first of October, can it?' Klara said. 'We've only just had midsummer, which means we have three months before then. If you let me go to Stockholm and find work I promise you the cottage will stay in your possession.'

When he heard these words the colour drained from Jan's face and his head fell back as if he were about to pass out.

It was so wonderful of the little girl. This was what he had been waiting for the whole time. But how would he survive if she were to go away and leave him?

Storsnipa

Jan from Skrolycka was walking along the same forest path he and his womenfolk had taken on their way home from church a couple of hours earlier. Then they had been happy and content.

Kattrinna and Jan had just had a long discussion and they'd agreed that before sending their daughter away or, indeed, doing anything at all, Jan should go and ask Karl Karlsson, who attended parliament as the Riksdag man for Storvik, whether Lars Gunnarsson had the right to take their cottage from them.

There was no one in the whole parish of Svartsjö as knowledgeable about law and regulations as the Riksdag man for Storvik. People wise enough to turn to him for help in matters of land rights or purchase, deeds of inventory, auctions or drawing up wills, could be certain that everything would be done in full accordance with the law and there would be no chance of conflicts and lawsuits arising later.

But Karl Karlsson was a gruff and commanding figure with a stern appearance and a harsh voice, and Jan was not very happy about having to talk to him. 'The first thing he'll do when I arrive is give me a dressing-down for not having any documents,' he thought. 'There are lots of people he has frightened so badly at the start that they haven't had the courage to go on and tell him what they wanted advice about.'

Jan had set off from home in such haste that he hadn't given any thought to the terrifying man he was on his way to meet. But once he was walking through the Askedalarna pastures on the path up to the forest his old fears returned to him. It was foolish of him not to have taken Klara with him.

He hadn't seen her when he was leaving home. She may, perhaps, have slipped off to some lonely spot in the forest to cry her sorrows away? She never wanted anyone to see her when she was upset.

As Jan was about to branch off into the forest he heard the sound of singing up on the hillside to his right.

He stopped and listened. It was a woman singing, but could it really be the person whose voice he thought it resembled? Surely not?

Before continuing on his way he wanted to find out what was going on. He could hear the song quite clearly, but the singer was hidden by the trees. He turned off the track and pushed his way through thickets, trying to locate her.

She wasn't as close as he'd thought. Nor did she stay in one place, and he followed her as she moved farther and farther away. Farther away and ever higher, until he thought the singing was coming from directly overhead.

It seemed certain that whoever was singing must be making her way up Storsnipa.

He realised she had taken a path that wound its way up the hill where the slope was almost vertical. The path was bordered by a dense growth of young birch trees that made it quite impossible for him to see her. In spite of the steepness of the path she was moving uphill quickly and he felt she was ascending with the speed of a bird on the wing, singing all the while.

Jan took a less steep route up the hill but, having left the path in his eagerness, he had to struggle through dense forest and it was hardly surprising that he was left far behind. Moreover, he felt a heavy weight in his chest and was finding it more and more difficult to breathe as he followed and listened to the song.

In the end his progress was so slow that he scarcely seemed to be moving.

It is not always easy to recognise voices and it becomes even more difficult in the forest because there are so many other sounds – all the rustles and murmurs – that seem to join in the song. But he felt compelled to go far enough to catch a glimpse of the young woman who was so happy that she was almost flying up the steep slope. Otherwise he felt doubt and suspicion would be with him for the rest of his days.

And he also knew that if he could reach the top of the hill certainty would be his, for the summit was empty and bare and whoever was singing would have nowhere to hide from him.

There had been a time when Storsnipa, too, had been covered with forest, but twenty or more years ago a forest fire had swept across the wide crest of the hill and it had remained bare ever since. Heather and crowberry and Iceland moss had slowly crept over the rocks and slabs, but there were still no trees to offer concealment.

The view from the top was magnificent since the forest had gone. The full length of Lake Löven was visible, and the whole green valley around the lake as well as the blue mountains that sheltered the valley. When the young people of Askedalarna climbed to the heights of Storsnipa from their narrow valley, it made them think of the mountain to which the Devil took Our Lord Jesus to show him the kingdoms of the world in all their splendour.

The instant Jan finally put the forest behind him and emerged into the open he saw the singer. A cairn had been built on the very highest point, where the view was at its widest, and on the topmost rock of that cairn stood Klara Fina Goldenborg in her red dress. She stood out clearly against the pale evening sky, and if the people down in the valleys and forests far below had turned their eyes up to Storsnipa, they would have been able to see her standing there in her bright dress.

She was gazing out across mile upon mile of the country. She could see white churches on steep little hills by the shores of lakes, ironworks and manor houses nestling in parks and gardens, a long unbroken line of farms along the edge of the forest, the patchwork of cultivated fields, long winding roads and forests that had no end.

At first she sang, but she soon fell silent and thought only of the great, open world that lay before her eyes.

And then she threw her arms open wide. It was as if she wanted to embrace it all, all the grandeur, immensity and richness from which she had been excluded until this day.

*

Jan did not arrive home until far into the night and when he did so he was unable to give an account of anything. He claimed to have visited the Riksdag man and talked to him, but he was unable to remember what advice they had been given.

'It's not worth our while to do anything,' he repeated time after time. And that was all Kattrinna could get from him.

Jan walked bent low and looked as if he was at death's door. His coat was stained with moss and earth. Kattrinna asked whether he had fallen and hurt himself.

No, he had not, but he must have lain on the ground for a while, that was for sure.

Was he ill, then?

No, not that. It was just that something had come to a stop.

But whatever it was that stopped at the moment he understood that his little girl was not offering to save their cottage from love, but from a desire to go out into the world and leave them – whatever it was that had stopped, he did not want to say.

The Eve of Departure

On the eve of Klara Fina Goldenborg's departure for Stockholm, her father Jan found an endless succession of jobs he had to do. As soon as he came home from his day's work he had to go up to the forest for wood. Then he set about mending a bar on the gate – it had been hanging down broken for at least a year – and when that job was finished he began sorting and organising his fishing gear.

And all the time he was thinking how strange it was that he wasn't feeling any real sorrow. He had become again the same man he had been eighteen years earlier. He could not be happy and he could not be sad. As he stood watching Klara on the summit of Storsnipa opening her arms wide to embrace the whole world, his heart had stopped, just like a clock that has taken a violent knock.

It was like the time years before when everyone wanted him to be pleased about the baby that was on its way. But he hadn't asked to have her. He really had not. And now everyone was expecting him to be miserable and depressed, but he wasn't.

The cottage was full of people who had come to say goodbye to Klara. It would be nothing short of embarrassing to go in and let them see that he was neither weeping nor wailing. Better to stay outside.

In any case, it was as well from his point of view that things had happened as they had happened. If things had remained as before he did not know how he could have borne the longing and grief.

When he walked past the window he saw that the cottage was decorated with greenery and there were coffee cups on the table, just as on that other day he had been remembering. Kattrinna had wanted to have a small celebration for a daughter who was going out into the world to save their home.

There were tears in the cottage, for sure, both in the eyes of those who lived there and those who had come to say goodbye. Even out in the yard he could hear the sound of Klara weeping, but it meant nothing to him.

'Dear people,' he mumbled as he stood there, 'this is just as it should be. Just consider nestlings. If they will not leave willingly, they are pushed out of the nest. Have you seen a young cuckoo? What could be worse than seeing him lying in the nest, big and fat and screaming for food while his foster-parents exhaust themselves for his sake?

'No, everything is good as it is. The young cannot just remain at home as a burden on the old. They have to go out into the world. That's what they must do, my dear people.'

Eventually the cottage fell silent. All the neighbours must have departed and he could risk going in.

But he carried on fiddling with his fishing gear a while longer. What he really wanted was for both Kattrinna and Klara to be in bed asleep before he crossed the threshold.

When he hadn't heard a sound for some considerable time he crept up to the cottage as quietly as a thief.

But the women had not gone to bed yet. As he walked past the open window he saw Klara. She was sitting with her arms outstretched across the table and with her face resting on them. It looked as if she was crying.

Kattrinna was standing farther into the room. She was just folding her big shawl around Klara's bundle of clothes.

'You can stop that, Mother,' the girl said without raising her head. 'Surely you can see that Father is angry with me for leaving?'

'He'll get over it, I know he will,' Kattrinna said calmly.

'You're just saying that because you don't care about him,' Klara continued, still sobbing. 'You're only thinking of the cottage. But you must see that Father and I are one. I won't leave him!'

'And the cottage?'

'I don't care about the cottage. All I care about is for Father to love me again.'

Jan walked quietly away from the door and sat down on the doorstep. He did not believe that Klara would stay at home, indeed, he knew better than anyone else that she had to leave. But, still, he felt as if that soft little bundle had been laid in his arms once more. His heart began working again, and now it was beating as if it had been stopped for years and had to make up for lost time.

All at once he knew that now he had neither shield nor defence.

Sorrow came, and yearning came. He saw them as black shadows over under the trees.

He opened his arms and spread them wide, and a happy smile came to his face.

'Welcome! Welcome! Welcome!' he said.

On the Landing Stage

When the steamer *Anders Fryxell* drew away from Borg Landing with Klara Fina Goldenborg on board, Jan and Kattrinna stood and gazed after it until there was no longer any sign of the ship or the girl. The rest of the people who'd had business at the landing stage dispersed. The agent lowered the flag and closed the depot, but the two of them remained.

It was understandable that they stayed as long as they thought the ship was in sight, but why they did not leave afterwards was something they barely understood themselves.

Perhaps it was just that they were afraid to go home to an empty cottage with only one another for company.

'Now he is the only one I have to cook for,' Kattrinna thought, 'the only one I have to wait for. But what do I care about him? He might just as well have gone too. Really! The lass was the one who understood him and his nonsense, not me. I'd be better off on my own.'

'It would have been easier to go home with my sorrow if I didn't have that old sourpuss Kattrinna there,' Jan thought. 'Klara knew how to deal with her and get her to be gentle and happy, but I'm not likely to get a kind word out of her from now on.'

But then, all of a sudden, Jan jumped. He bent forward and slapped his knees in surprise. A new light came into his eyes and his whole face lit up.

His gaze remained fixed on the water and Kattrinna couldn't help thinking he was seeing something remarkable there even though she, standing beside him, couldn't make anything out. All she could see were the small, grey-green waves chasing one another across the surface in a never-ending game.

Jan ran out along the landing stage as far as he could and bent down over the water. The expression on his face was the one it always took on when Klara was coming to him. It was an expression he never had when talking to anyone else.

His mouth opened and his lips twitched but no words reached Kattrinna. One smile after another passed across his face, just as when the girl was there, joking with him.

'Jan, Jan,' Kattrinna said. 'What's got into you?'

He didn't answer, just gestured with his hand for her to be quiet.

Then, all at once, he straightened up slightly and it looked as if his eyes were following something that was moving away across the small grey waves.

Whatever he was watching was moving away quickly in the same direction the steamship had taken a little while before. Jan was no longer bending forward, he was now standing fully upright, his hand shading his eyes in order to see better.

He remained like that until it seemed there was nothing more to see. Then he turned to Kattrinna and went right up to her.

'I don't expect you saw anything, did you?' he said.

'What was there to see except the lake and the waves?' she asked back.

'The little girl! She came rowing back,' he said, lowering his voice to no more than a whisper. 'The captain let her borrow a boat. I saw that it had the same badge as the steamship. She said she had forgotten something when she left – something she wanted to talk to us about.'

'Jan, dear Jan, you don't know what you're saying!' Kattrinna said. 'If the lass had come back I would have seen her too, wouldn't I?'

'Hush now and I'll tell you what she wanted of us!' Jan whispered in a voice that was solemn and mysterious. 'The fact is she was worried about how things will be between the two of us. In the past, she said, everything worked well because she was the go-between, taking me in one hand and you in the other. But she didn't know what would happen now that she wasn't there to keep us together. What she said was, "Perhaps Mother and Father will each go their own way now."'

'Heavens above, what made her think of that?' Kattrinna said. She was so gripped by the words, which reflected her own thoughts, that she forgot how impossible it was for their daughter to have rowed back to the landing place and spoken to her husband without her noticing.

'"So I've come back to put your hands together and, for my sake, you mustn't let go. You must hold on tight until I return home and can take each of you by the hand as I used to." As soon as she'd said that she rowed away again.'

There was silence for a while on the landing stage.

'And here is my hand now,' Jan said in an uncertain voice, as if he was both anxious and shy. He held out his hand, which had always remained amazingly soft however hard he worked. 'Because our girl wants it,' he added.

'And here is mine,' Kattrinna said. 'I don't understand what you have seen, but if you and our daughter want us to stay together, that's what I want too.'

Then the two of them walked hand in hand the whole way home to the cottage.

The Letter

One morning a couple of weeks after Klara from Skrolycka had left, her father Jan was mending the fence in the grazing land closest to the forest. In fact, it was close enough for him to hear the murmuring of the trees and to see the hen capercaillie pecking around under the trees with a long row of chicks following her.

He had almost finished the job when he heard a loud roar from farther up the hill. It sounded so dreadful that his first sensation was one of fear.

He stood still and listened and soon he heard it again, but on hearing it for a second time he realised it was nothing to be frightened of. Quite the opposite, in fact, it was almost certainly someone calling for help.

He threw aside his withies and poles and set off through the copse of birch trees into the darkness of the spruce forest. He didn't have to go far before he saw what the trouble was. There was a big dangerous bog up there and, just as he had feared, one of the Falla cows was sinking in the quagmire.

He recognised at once that it was the best cow in the herd, a cow for which Lars Gunnarsson had been offered two hundred riksdaler.

She was already deep in the mire and was now so frightened that she was lying still and lowing weakly at long intervals. But he could see how she had struggled. Mud was splashed up over her horns and she had torn up tussocks of green moss over a wide area.

Jan thought her bellowing had been so loud that it would have been heard all over Askedalarna, but as it was, he was the only one who had come up to the bog. As soon as he realised what was happening, he ran down to the farm without a moment's hesitation to fetch help.

The work of laying planks and poles over the bog and getting ropes under the cow to winch her out was long and slow. She had sunk right down to her back and only her head was still above the mud when they reached her.

Once the cow was back on firm ground at last and they had taken her down to Falla, a message came from the farmer's wife that all the men who had struggled to save the cow were invited in for coffee.

No one had worked harder or been keener to rescue the cow than Jan from Skrolycka and it was thanks to him that the cow had been rescued at all. And we should remember that this was a cow worth at least two hundred riksdaler!

This was a huge stroke of luck for Jan. It was unthinkable that the new owners of the farm would ignore a deed of this sort. Something similar had happened back in the days of the previous farmer, when a horse had torn itself on a fence. The man who found the horse and arranged for it to be brought back to the farm had been given ten riksdaler by Farmer Erik even though the horse was so badly injured that Erik had to shoot it.

This cow, however, was alive and hadn't suffered any injuries. It seemed quite obvious that by the following day Jan would be in a position to go to the cantor – or someone else who could write – and ask him to write a letter to Klara telling her to come home.

So when Jan went into the Falla farmhouse there is no doubt he was holding his head high. The old woman, Farmer Erik's widow, was going round pouring coffee and Jan wasn't surprised when she served him his coffee even before Lars Gunnarsson was given his.

While drinking their coffee they all talked about how quick and capable Jan had been. The only ones who said nothing were the new owner and his wife, neither of whom uttered a single word of praise.

But since Jan was quite sure the bad times were over and fortune was now smiling on him, he had no difficulty in finding cause for comfort and consolation. It could be, couldn't it, that Lars was staying silent so that his words would have all the more force when he did speak?

Lars was certainly taking his time about voicing any praise and the other people present were beginning to grow quiet and look a little embarrassed.

When the old farmer's widow went round offering to top up the coffee cups many of them – Jan included – had to be coaxed. But she said to him: 'Oh, do have some more, Jan. If you hadn't been so quick-witted today we should have lost a cow worth two hundred riksdaler.'

This was followed by a profound silence. All eyes turned to the new owner, everyone expecting that there would be a word of thanks from him too.

Lars cleared his throat several times as if to ensure that what he was going to say would emerge with sufficient emphasis.

'It seems to me there is something more than a little strange about this business,' he said. 'We all know that Jan owes two hundred riksdaler and we all know that I was offered exactly that sum for Star last spring. The fact that Star went down in the bog today and that Jan was the one to save her is – it has to be said – very convenient for Jan.'

Lars fell silent and cleared his throat again. Jan stood up and went closer, but neither he nor anyone else had an answer ready.

'I don't know how it came about that Jan of all people happened to be the one to hear the cow up in the bog,' Lars Gunnarsson continued. 'Perhaps he was closer to where the accident occurred than he is prepared to admit. Perhaps he saw a chance to escape his debt – he might even have been the one who drove the cow ...'

At this point Jan's fist struck the table with such force that the coffee cups jumped off their saucers.

'You judge others by your own standards, you do,' Jan said. 'That's the sort of thing you would do, but not me. But let me tell you something – I'm keeping an eye on your dirty tricks. That day last winter ...'

Jan was about to say something that could only have resulted in the farmer becoming his irreconcilable enemy when the widow of the old Falla farmer tugged his sleeve.

'Careful now, Jan!' she said.

Jan followed her advice. Then he saw Kattrinna coming across the farmyard with a letter in her hand.

It must be the letter from Klara they had been longing for ever since she left. Kattrinna knew how happy he would be and that was why she was bringing it.

Jan looked around in a confused sort of way. There were many angry words burning on the tip of his tongue, but he no longer had time for them. What did it matter if he took revenge on Lars Gunnarsson? What did it matter if he defended himself or not? The letter was drawing him with a power he couldn't resist. Before the people in the farmhouse had recovered from their fear of the accusations he had been about to hurl at the farmer, Jan had left the house and gone out to Kattrinna.

August Där Nol

Klara from Skrolycka had been gone for a month or so when August Där Nol from Prästerud came to Aske-dalarna one evening.

He had been a schoolmate of Klara's at Östanby School for many years and they had been confirmed the same summer. He was a fine, serious boy with a good reputation. His parents were well-off and he could look forward to a less troubled and better future than most other people.

He had been away for the last six months and it was only on his return that he learnt that Klara had gone out into the world to earn two hundred riksdaler.

It was his mother who told him the story and even before she had finished he picked up his cap and was on his way. He did not stop until he reached the gate leading into the small green plot at Skrolycka.

Having got there, he did not walk on past, he just stood there looking at the cottage.

Kattrinna noticed him standing there and made an excuse of fetching water from the spring, but he did not greet her or show any sign of wanting to speak to her.

A while later Jan came down from the forest with a bundle of wood under his arm. When August Där Nol saw him approaching the gate he moved aside, but once Jan had gone through, August returned to his former position.

After he'd been standing there a while longer, the cottage window opened. It was no more than a couple of arms' lengths away, so he could see Jan sitting on one side of the window with his pipe and Kattrinna sitting on the other with her knitting.

'Well now, dear Kattrinna,' Jan said. 'Here we are of an evening and things are pretty good for us. There is only one thing I would wish for, though.'

'There are a hundred things I would wish for,' Kattrinna said. 'And even if I was given all of them, I still wouldn't be satisfied.'

'All I want is for the net maker to visit, or anyone else who can read,' Jan said. 'They could read Klara's letter to us.'

'You've heard that letter so often since it came that you can recite it off by heart word perfect,' Kattrinna answered.

'That's true,' Jan said. 'But it's still nice to hear someone read it out. It makes me feel that the little girl is standing here talking to me, and I can see her shining eyes with every word I hear.'

'Well, I've nothing against hearing it again,' Kattrinna said, looking out of the window. 'But on a nice bright evening like this everyone is likely to be off somewhere else and we can't expect anyone to come to our cottage.'

'Listening to Klara's letter while I smoke my pipe would be sweeter than a bun with my coffee,' Jan said. 'But I suppose I've driven everyone in Askedalarna to distraction asking them to read me the letter. I don't know who to turn to next.'

A moment later Jan jumped with surprise. The words were barely out of his mouth when the door opened and August Där Nol appeared on the threshold.

'Lord above! You must have been sent by Heaven, August, my dear fellow,' Jan said once he'd said hello and asked the visitor to sit down. 'I have a letter here which I'd like you to read to us old folks. It's from a schoolmate of yours. I expect you'd like to hear how she's getting on?'

August Där Nol took the letter gently and read it aloud. He spoke the words slowly, as if drinking them in.

When he'd finished, Jan said:

'You read wonderfully well, dear August. I've never heard Klara's words sound as beautiful as they do from your lips. Would you give me the pleasure of reading it once more?'

The boy read the letter aloud for the second time, just as reverently as before. It was as if he were quenching his thirst at a refreshing spring.

When he finished he folded the letter and smoothed it with his hand. He was about to hand it back, but he must have thought he hadn't folded it neatly enough and so he did it again.

Then he sat in utter silence. Jan attempted unsuccessfully to start a conversation and eventually the boy stood up to leave.

'It's good when someone helps you out,' Jan said. 'And there's something else I'd like help with. We have a kitten here – it's actually Klara's. We can't afford to keep it and ought to put it down, but I can't bring myself to do it and Kattrinna – well, she hasn't the heart to drown it either. We were just saying we'd have to talk to someone about it.'

August Där Nol stammered a few words that no one could hear.

'Put the kitten in a basket, Kattrinna, will you?' Jan continued. 'August can take it away with him and deal with it so we never have to see it again.'

His wife picked up a small white kitten that was sleeping on the bed, put it in an old basket, tied a cloth over the top and handed it to the poor lad.

'I'm glad to be rid of the kitten,' Jan said. 'It's so jolly and lively, it's much too like Klara herself. Best be rid of it.'

August Där Nol walked to the door without saying a word, but all of a sudden he turned round, took Jan's hand and squeezed it.

'Thank you!' he said. 'You have given me more than you can ever know.'

'That's what you think, my dear fellow,' Jan said to himself once the boy had gone. 'I know about these things, I do. I know what I have given you, and I know who it was who taught me.'

The First of October

On the first of October Jan at Skrolycka spent the whole afternoon lying fully dressed on his bed. His face was turned to the wall and it was impossible to get a word out of him.

That morning he and Kattrinna had gone down to the landing stage to meet the little girl. It wasn't that she had written to say she was coming, she hadn't, but Jan had come to the conclusion that this was the way it would happen.

It was, after all, the first of October, the day the money was due to Lars Gunnarsson and therefore also the day Klara would arrive home with the money. He wasn't expecting her to come before then, as she would obviously need to stay in Stockholm as long as possible in order to earn such a large sum. But nor did he believe she would be away longer than that, for if she hadn't managed to scrape the money together, she had no reason to stay there once the first of October was past.

While he was waiting on the landing stage Jan had told himself that when his little girl caught sight of them from the boat she would put on a sad face and when she came ashore she would immediately tell them she'd been unable to come up with that much money.

When she had said that, both Jan and Kattrinna would pretend they took her at her word: Jan would say that he couldn't understand how she dared come home since she must know that he and Kattrinna were only interested in the money.

But he was absolutely certain that before they left the landing stage she would produce a thick wallet from the pocket of her skirt and hand it to them.

What he then intended to do was to let Kattrinna take the money and count it while he would just stand and gaze at Klara.

He was certain she would notice that the only thing that mattered to him was that she had come home, and she would probably tell him he was just as silly now as when she left.

That is how Jan had dreamt their reunion would be. But his dream had not come to pass.

He and Kattrinna did not need to wait very long on the landing stage that day. The boat arrived in good time, and when it arrived it was so packed with goods and people for the big market in Broby that it had been impossible at first to see whether Klara was on board.

Jan had expected her to be the first to come running down the gangway, but a couple of men came instead. When there was still no sign of her, Jan tried to find her on the steamboat, but he couldn't get through the crowd. He was so sure she was somewhere on board, however, that when they began to pull in the gangplank he shouted to the captain that the boat must not depart as there was still one passenger to come ashore.

The captain asked the crew, who said there were no more passengers due to disembark at Svartsjö, and then the boat sailed. So that was that and he and Kattrinna walked home alone. As soon as they reached the cottage he threw himself down on the bed, so worn and weary that he didn't know where he'd find the strength to get up again.

The people of Askedalarna had seen them returning from the boat without Klara and there was much speculation as to how it would all end. One after another their neighbours found excuses to go over to Skrolycka to enquire about the situation.

Was it true that Klara hadn't been on the boat? Was it also true that they hadn't received a letter or heard a word from her through the whole of September?

Jan did not respond to any of the questions. Not a single word. It didn't matter who came, he just lay there motionless.

Kattrinna was the one who had to talk to them, in so far

as she knew anything. The neighbours probably assumed that Jan was lying where he was lying because he was so depressed at having to leave the cottage. Well, they were welcome to believe that, but he wasn't in the least concerned about the cottage.

His wife was weeping and wailing and the visitors, once they were there, felt they had to stay in order to show their sympathy and offer what words of comfort they could come up with.

Surely it was impossible for Lars Gunnarsson to take their cottage? The old farmer's widow at Falla wouldn't allow it, would she? She had always been a fair and honest person.

And the day wasn't over yet. They might still hear from Klara before it was too late. That, of course, depended on whether she had succeeded in earning two hundred riksdaler in the space of three short months. But that girl had always had such unbelievable good fortune, hadn't she?

They sat there discussing the possibilities for and against. Kattrinna reminded them that Klara would have been unable to earn anything during her first weeks. She had lodged with people from Svartsjö who had moved to Stockholm, but she'd had to pay her way while she was with them.

Then, however, she'd a great stroke of luck in that she met the same pedlar who'd given her the red dress. He had helped her find work.

Was there also a possibility that he had provided her with money, too? It wasn't impossible, was it?

No, it certainly wasn't impossible, Kattrinna told them, but Klara had neither come home nor sent a letter, which must mean she had failed.

The visitors to the cottage grew more anxious and fearful with every minute that passed. They could feel in their bones that something dreadful was about to happen to the people who lived there.

When the mood was at its lowest, the door opened and in came a man who had rarely been seen in Askedalarna before. He wasn't a man much given to visiting out-of-the-way places of that kind.

When he entered, the cottage fell silent and still – the sort of silence that reigns in the forest during the nights of winter. All eyes followed him, except Jan's. He, Jan that is, did not move even though Kattrinna whispered to him that Karl Karlsson, the Riksdag man from Storvik, had come to their cottage.

Karl Karlsson had a rolled-up document in his hand and everyone took for granted that he had been sent by the new owner of Falla to tell the Skrolycka folk what their fate was now that they were unable to pay the sum he was demanding.

Karl Karlsson was the focus of many worried eyes, but since his face wore its usual expression of authority, it was impossible for anyone to work out the severity of the blow he had come to deliver.

He shook hands with Kattrinna first and then with all the others. One by one they stood up to greet him, Jan being the only one not to move.

'I am not especially familiar with this district,' the Riksdag man said. 'But I take it that this is the place called Skrolycka in Askedalarna?'

Yes, it was indeed, and they all nodded in answer to his question, though not one of them seemed capable of uttering a word. In fact, they were amazed that Kattrinna had sufficient presence of mind to nudge Börje to stand up and give the visitor somewhere to sit.

He pulled his chair up to the table, where he placed his rolled-up paper before taking out a snuff-box and placing it beside the paper. Then it was time for his spectacles to come out of their case and be polished with a blue checked handkerchief.

Having proceeded thus far with his preparations he again looked at them one by one. They were all just very ordinary, humble folk, so much so that he didn't have any idea of names and who was who.

'I'm here to talk to Jan Andersson of Skrolycka,' he said.

'That's him, lying over there,' the net maker said, pointing to the bed.

'Is he ill?' Karl Karlsson asked.

'Oh no,' several people said at the same time.

'And he isn't drunk either,' Börje added.

'And he's not asleep either,' the net maker said.

'He walked so far today that he's tired,' Kattrinna said, thinking it best to explain the situation in that way.

At the same time she bent over her husband and tried to make him get up.

But Jan remained where he was.

'Can he understand what I'm saying?' the Riksdag man asked.

'Oh yes, he'll understand,' they all assured him.

'I doubt if he's expecting a visitor like Karl Karlsson, the Riksdag man from Storvik, to be the bearer of good news,' the net maker said.

The visitor turned his head and looked at the net maker's small, red-rimmed eyes.

'Oh, it's you, is it, Ol Bengtsa from Ljusterbyn? You haven't always been afraid to meet Karl Karlsson, have you?' he said.

Then he turned back to the table and began reading a letter.

All the rest of them were utterly astonished. His voice had been so friendly – indeed, you could almost say he'd given a little smile.

'The situation is this,' Karl Karlsson said. 'A few days ago I received a letter from someone calling herself Klara Fina Goldenborg Jansdotter from Skrolycka. In her letter she says she has left home to earn the two hundred riksdaler her parents are supposed to pay to Lars Gunnarsson of Falla on the first of October in order to acquire ownership rights to the land on which their cottage is built.'

He paused at this point to make it easier for his listeners to follow his presentation.

'She has sent moneys to me,' he continued, 'and requested me to come to Askedalarna and settle the matter properly with the new owner of Falla Farm in such a manner that he cannot come up with further difficulties at a later date. She is a clever lass, this one,' he said, folding the letter. 'She came to me right from the start. If everyone did what she has done, things in this parish would be better for it.'

Before the visitor had finished speaking, Jan sat up on the edge of the bed.

'And the girl?' he said. 'Where is she?'

'What I now need is confirmation that her parents agree with their daughter that I should be entrusted with concluding ...'

'But the girl, the girl?' Jan interrupted him. 'Where is the girl?'

'Where is she?' the Riksdag man said, looking through the letter. 'She says it hasn't been possible for her to earn all this money in just a few months. But she has a job with a kind lady who has allowed her an advance. She has to stay there now until she has worked off what she owes.'

'She's not coming home then?' Jan said.

'No, not in the immediate future, as far as I can see,' the visitor said.

Jan lay back down on the bed and turned to the wall as before.

What did he care about the cottage and the rest of the business? What did he care whether he lived or not, when his little girl wasn't coming back?'

The Dream Begins

In the weeks that followed the visit of Karl Karlsson Jan was unable to do a thing. He just lay in bed grieving.

Every morning he would rise and put on his clothes with the intention of going to Falla and doing his day's work, but even before he was out of the door he felt so weak and exhausted that there was nothing for it but to go back and lie down.

Kattrinna tried to be patient with him, for she knew that pining – just like other ailments – had to be given time if it was to pass. But she did wonder how long it would take for Jan's yearning for Klara to ease. Was he still going to be lying in bed at Christmas, or even for the whole winter?

And it might have turned out like that if the old net maker hadn't dropped in to Skrolycka one evening to find out how things were and been asked to stay for a cup of coffee.

The net maker was always taciturn, the sort of fellow whose thoughts are far away and who doesn't really pay much attention to what is going on nearby. But once the coffee had been poured and he had emptied his into the saucer to let it cool, he obviously thought he should say something.

'I really do think a letter from Klara will come today. At last. I can feel it in my bones,' he said.

'But we had news of her just a fortnight ago in the letter to the Riksdag man,' Kattrinna answered.

The net maker blew on his coffee a couple of times before saying anything else. Then he thought it time once more to say a few words to fill the long silence.

'Well, it could be that something nice has happened, giving her something to write about.'

'What could possibly be nice?' Kattrinna said. 'When you're slaving away in service one day is much the same as another.'

The net maker bit off a piece of sugar and swallowed his coffee in big gulps. When he'd finished, a deep silence fell on the cottage – so deep that he found it little short of horrifying.

'Klara might have met somebody on the street, mightn't she?' he suggested, his dull eyes staring listlessly straight ahead. It was difficult to believe that he actually knew what he was saying.

Kattrinna didn't think this called for an answer, so she refilled his cup and said nothing.

'It could be that the person she met was an old woman who had difficulty walking and this woman fell over just as Klara was passing,' the net maker continued in the same absent tone as before.

'Would that really be something worth writing home about?' Kattrinna said, sounding tired of the way he was keeping on.

'Yes, but what if Klara stopped and helped her up,' the net maker said, 'and the old woman was so glad of her help that she took out her purse there and then and gave the girl no less than ten riksdaler! Surely that would be something worth talking about?'

'It certainly would,' Kattrinna said, sounding more than a little impatient. 'If it were true. But as it is, it's just something you are making up as you go along.'

'You have to be able to find some pleasure in your imagination if you are to keep going,' the net maker said apologetically. 'It usually leaves a better taste than the real thing, it does.'

'Yes, you'd know all about both, wouldn't you?' Kattrinna said.

Immediately after that the net maker went on his way and once he was gone, Kattrinna gave no further thought to the whole business.

As for Jan, in the beginning he, too, took this to be no more than idle chatter. But lying there in bed doing nothing, he began to wonder whether the net maker's words might not conceal a hidden meaning.

There'd been a strange tone to his voice when talking about the letter, hadn't there? Would he really be bothered to invent a long tale like that just to have something to say? Perhaps he really had heard something? Perhaps he'd received a letter from Klara?

It was quite possible, wasn't it, that she'd had a great stroke of luck and was afraid to send the news directly to her parents. It was quite possible she had written to the net maker and asked him to prepare the ground. Perhaps that was what he had been trying to do this evening and they hadn't understood.

'He'll come again tomorrow,' Jan thought, 'and then we'll hear the whole truth.'

But for whatever reason the net maker did not come back the following day, nor the day after that. By the third day Jan's desire was so strong that he rose from bed and went over to his neighbour's cottage to find out whether there was any meaning behind his words.

The old man was alone, working on an old net he'd been given to mend. He was pleased that Jan had come. His gout was so bad, he said, that he'd been unable to leave home the last few days.

Jan did not want to ask him straight out whether he'd received a letter from Klara. He thought it would be easier for him to work his way round to the topic by the same method the other man had used.

'I've been thinking about what you said about Klara when you were up with us recently,' he said.

The old net maker looked up from his work. It took him a while to understand what Jan was referring to.

'Oh, that was just a little something I made up,' he said.

Jan moved closer to him.

'It was nice to hear it, all the same,' he said. 'Maybe there was more you could have said if Kattrinna hadn't been so mistrustful?'

'I suppose so,' the net maker said. 'It's about the only kind of amusement we can afford to help pass the time here in

Askedalarna.'

'I've been thinking,' Jan said, emboldened by the net maker's encouragement, 'that maybe the story didn't end with the old lady giving Klara ten riksdaler. Perhaps she also invited her to come and visit?'

'She might have,' the net maker said.

'Perhaps she was so rich that she owned a house. A whole house! Built of stone!' Jan suggested.

'That's not such a bad suggestion, Jan,' the old net maker said approvingly.

'And perhaps the rich lady is paying off Klara's debt?' Jan said. But then he stopped, because the net maker's daughter-in-law came into the room and he didn't want her to be party to their secret.

'I see you are up and about today, Jan,' she said. 'I'm glad you are feeling better.'

'And Ol Bengtsa here is the one I have to thank for it, kind fellow that he is,' Jan said in a mysterious tone of voice. 'He's the one who cured me.'

With that Jan said goodbye and departed. The old net maker sat there and stared after him for a long time.

'I don't know what he means when he says I cured him, Lisa,' he said to his daughter-in-law. 'Do you think he could be going ...'

Inherited Treasures

L ater in the autumn Jan was making his way home from Falla Farm where he had spent the day threshing. Since his conversation with the net maker, he had felt like going back to work. He felt he had to do what he could to keep himself going. When his little girl came home, he didn't want her to face the shame of parents who'd been reduced to parish paupers.

When Jan had gone far enough to be out of sight of the windows of the farm, a woman came walking towards him. It was already growing dark, but Jan immediately recognised the farmer's wife – not the new one, who was married to Lars Gunnarsson, but the old one, the true Falla farmer's wife.

She was wearing a large shawl that reached right down to the hem of her skirts. Jan had never seen her so well wrapped up before and he wondered if she was ill. She hadn't been looking at all well recently. When Farmer Erik died back in the spring she hadn't had a white hair on her head but now, just half a year later, Jan thought there was scarcely any black hair left.

She stopped and greeted him and then they stood there talking. She didn't say anything that might suggest she had come out just to meet Jan, but he sensed that was her intention. It suddenly occurred to him that she might want to talk about Klara, and he was more than a little disappointed when she began talking about something quite different.

'Tell me, Jan,' she said, 'do you remember the old owner of Falla, my father, who had the farm before Erik came?'

'Of course I remember him,' Jan said. 'I must have been at least twelve by the time he died.'

'He had a good son-in-law,' the old farmer's widow said.

'Yes, he certainly did,' Jan agreed.

She said nothing for a while but then, after sighing several times, she began speaking.

'There's something I should have consulted you about, Jan. You aren't the sort to go gossiping to right and left about what I'm about to say, are you?'

'No, I can hold my tongue, I can.'

'Yes, I think I've noticed that this year.'

Jan's mind filled with renewed hope. It wasn't unreasonable to think that Klara had turned to the Falla widow and asked her to pass on to her parents news of the great good fortune that had happened to her.

The old net maker had suffered a severe attack of gout immediately after the conversation interrupted by his daughter-in-law and he had been in such a bad way that Jan hadn't been able to talk to him for weeks. He was up again now, but still very weak, and the worst thing of all was that he seemed to have lost his memory after his illness. Jan had been waiting for him to bring up Klara's letter of his own accord, but he hadn't done so, and when he didn't respond to a number of hints, Jan had asked him directly.

The old man claimed he had never received a letter. He had gone so far as to pull out the drawer in the table and raise the lid of his clothes' chest to demonstrate to Jan that there was no letter.

He had obviously forgotten what he'd done with it, so it wasn't any wonder that Jan's little girl had turned to the Falla widow instead. It was just a pity she hadn't done so from the start.

The widow stood in silence and hesitated for quite some time, to the point where Jan became so sure he was right that he found it hard to follow her properly when she resumed talking about her father.

'Right at the end my father called Erik to his deathbed to thank him for having treated him so well, even though he had been too weak to be of any use for many years. "Don't even think of it, Father," Erik said. 'We are happy to keep you however long you choose to stay." That's what he said, and he meant it too.'

'Yes, there can be no doubt he meant it,' Jan said. 'There was nothing sly about Erik.'

'Patience now, Jan!' the Falla widow said. 'We are only going to talk about the old ones for a little while longer. Do you remember that long cane with the silver knob Father used to walk with?'

'I do – that and the tall cap he always wore to church.'

'So you remember his cap, too. Do you know what Father did while he was lying there? He sent me to fetch the cane and the cap and he gave them to Erik. "I could have given you something more valuable," he said, "but I'm giving you these because it will bring you greater honour to have things that everyone knows I used. They will act as a good testimonial."'

'They certainly did – and well-deserved too.'

As Jan was saying this he noticed that the widow was holding her shawl tight around her. She had something hidden under it, that was for sure, and it might be a message from Klara. She would get round to telling him, all in good time. All this talk about her father and the gifts was leading up to it.

'I've told the children about this many times – Lars Gunnarsson too,' the farmer's widow said. 'And when Erik was ill last spring I do believe that both Lars and Anna expected Lars to be called to the bed, just as Erik had been before. I had taken the things out so Erik would have them ready to hand if he wanted to give them to Lars. But he had no thought of doing so.'

Her voice was trembling and when she began speaking again she sounded anxious and hesitant.

'Once when we were alone I asked him what he wanted to do about it and he said that I could give the things to Lars when he was dead if I wanted to. He didn't have the strength to make a speech, he said.'

At this point the farmer's widow opened her big shawl and Jan could see she was concealing a long cane with a large silver knob and a stiff cap with a high crown.

'There are some words that are too heavy to utter,' she said with great solemnity. 'Just answer me with a gesture, if you will, Jan: can I give these things to Lars Gunnarsson?'

Jan took a step back. This was something he had put far behind him. It was so long since Farmer Erik had died that he scarcely remembered how it had happened.

'You do understand, Jan, that I don't want to know anything more than whether Lars should receive the cane and the cap with as much right as Erik did. And you are the one who knows, for you were with him in the forest.'

Then, when Jan remained silent, she added: 'It would be better for me if I could give them to Lars. If I did so, I think I would have an easier time with the young people at home.'

Her voice failed her again and Jan began to understand why she had grown so old. He himself was now so taken up with other things that he no longer remembered the thoughts he'd once had of vengeance against the new owner of the farm.

'Peace and forgiveness are the best things,' he said. 'They will take you farthest.'

The old woman took a deep breath before saying: 'I see, so that's what you think. Things were as I thought, then.' She straightened her back, drawing herself up as tall as could be. 'I shan't ask you how it happened. It's better for me to know nothing about it. But one thing is quite certain and that is that Lars Gunnarsson will never lay a hand on my father's cane.'

She had already turned to go when she came to a sudden stop.

'Listen to me, Jan,' she said. 'Take the cane and the cap with you. I want them to be in good and faithful hands. I daren't take them home with me because I might be forced to give them to Lars. Take them as a memory of your old master, who always meant well by you.'

Tall and proud, she walked away, leaving Jan standing there holding the cane and the cap. He scarcely understood how this had happened. He could never have expected an honour as great as this. Were these heirlooms really his now?

But then, all at once, the explanation came to him. Klara was behind this. The Falla widow knew his status would soon be so grand that nothing was too good for him. In fact, had the cane been solid silver and the cap solid gold, they would have been even more suitable for the man who was Klara's father.

Dressed in Silk

Neither father nor mother received a letter from Klara, but it was of no great importance now they knew she was staying silent simply in order to surprise them and bring them even greater joy when the time came for her to make her great news public.

Nevertheless, it was a good thing that Jan had been given a glimpse of what fate had in store for her, because otherwise he could easily have been made to look foolish by people who thought they knew more about Klara's path than he did.

Kattrinna's attendance at church was one example of this.

Kattrinna attended church on the first Sunday in Advent and on her return home she was both sad and fearful.

She had noticed a couple of young men who'd been doing building work in Stockholm during the autumn standing talking to other young people, both boys and girls. When Kattrinna saw them she wondered whether they might have news of Klara and she had gone over to them to ask.

Whatever they were talking about was obviously very amusing and the men, anyway, were laughing so loudly that Kattrinna actually thought it was rather inappropriate just outside the church. They must have realised that too, for when Kattrinna approached them they nudged one another and went quiet.

So she only heard a few words from one of the men who had his back to her and didn't see her coming.

'And can you believe it, she was dressed in silk!' he said.

That was when a young girl elbowed him so hard that he stopped abruptly. He looked round and his face went bright red when he saw Kattrinna standing immediately behind him.

But then he tossed his head and, raising his voice, said: 'What's the matter with you? Why shouldn't I say that the queen was dressed in silk?'

As soon as he uttered those words, all the young people roared with laughter even more loudly than before. Kattrinna just walked past them, unable to bring herself to ask about anything.

She was so worried when she came home from church that Jan very nearly decided to tell her the truth of Klara's situation, but he thought better of it and just asked her to tell him again what they had said about the queen.

She did so. 'But you do understand that they only said that to distract me,' she added.

Jan still said nothing, but he couldn't help giving a little smile.

'What are you thinking about?' Kattrinna said. 'You have a strange look on your face these days. You know what they really meant, don't you?'

'No, I certainly don't,' Jan said. 'But, dear Kattrinna, we should surely have enough faith in our little girl to believe that everything is going as it should?'

'I get so anxious ...'

'The time hasn't yet come for them to be told or for me to be told,' Jan interrupted. 'It will be Klara herself who asked them not to say anything to us, so we shall just keep calm and wait, Kattrinna, that's what we shall do.'

Stars

One fine day when the little girl from Skrolycka had been away for almost eight months, Daft-Ingborg strode into the barn at Falla while Jan was doing the threshing.

Daft-Ingborg was Jan's niece, though he seldom saw her because she was afraid of Kattrinna. It was probably to avoid meeting his wife that she had come to see him at Falla in the middle of his working day.

Jan wasn't overjoyed to see her. It wasn't that she was completely mad – she wasn't, but she was very muddled, and she talked and talked. Jan carried on swinging his flail without paying any attention to her.

'Stop threshing, Jan,' she said 'so that I can tell you what I dreamt about you last night.'

'Best for you to come back some other time, Ingborg,' Jan said. 'The moment Lars Gunnarsson hears me taking a break from threshing, he'll be here to see what's going on.'

'I'll be quick, really quick,' Daft-Ingborg said. 'You do remember, don't you, that I'm the quickest of all my brothers and sisters. Though they were so useless in every way, all of them, that it's not much to boast about.'

'You were going to tell me about a dream,' Jan reminded her.

'I'm coming to that! I'm coming to that! Don't be afraid. I understand, understand. Strict master at Falla, now, strict master. But don't get anxious because of me. You won't get into trouble because of me. No chance of that with someone as clever as me.'

Jan would have liked to hear what she had dreamt about him because, sure as he was of his own great hopes, he still sought confirmation wherever it was available. But Daft-Ingborg had now gone off into her own thoughts and once that happened it wasn't easy to stop her.

She came right up close to Jan, bent forward with every new sentence, screwed up her eyes, shook her head and talked so that the words sprayed from her lips.

'Don't be afraid,' she said. 'Would I come to talk to someone doing the threshing at Falla if I didn't know that the master had gone up to the forest and the master's wife gone to the village to sell butter? "Do not let them out of your sight," as it says in the catechism. I know that. I make sure not to come when they can see me.'

'Out of the way, now Ingborg!' Jan said. 'I might accidentally hit you with the flail.'

'Remember how you boys used to hit me in the old days!' she said. 'And I still get hit even now. But I was the clever one when the minister was testing us about God and Jesus. "Nobody can catch Ingborg out," the minister used to say, "she knows her stuff." And I'm really good friends with the little ladies at Lövdala Manor. I recite the whole catechism to them – the questions as well as the answers. What a memory I've got! I know the Bible and the whole of the hymn book and all of the dean's sermons. Do you want me to recite something to you or would you like me to sing?'

Jan went back to his threshing and did not respond.

But still she would not go. She sat down on a sheaf of straw, sang a hymn with almost twenty verses and followed it by reciting several chapters from the Bible. Then she left without saying goodbye and was away for quite a while. Then, all of a sudden, she was standing in the barn door again.

'Quiet now, quiet!' she said. 'Now we won't say anything apart from what we ought to say. Just quiet, though, quiet!'

She stuck her forefinger in the air and stood still, her eyes open.

'No other thoughts, no other thoughts!' she said. 'We'll stick to the point. Just keep that flail still now!'

She waited until Jan obeyed.

'You came to me in a dream last night, that's what

happened. You came to me and this is what I said: "Are you out walking, Jan from Askedalarna?" You said: "No, I'm called Jan from Yearningdalarna now." And I said: "Ah, I see. Welcome, that's where I have lived the whole of my life."'

She disappeared from the open door. Jan was baffled by her words. He didn't return to his work immediately, but stood there pondering.

A moment or so later she was back.

'Now I remember why I came here,' she said. 'I was going to show you my stars.'

On her arm she had a small basket wrapped in a cloth. As she struggled with the knot she kept talking.

'These are real stars, these are. People who live in Yearningdalarna don't make do with earthly things, they have to set out in search of stars. There's no other way. You'll have to go out and seek them now, you too.'

'Oh no, not me, Ingborg,' Jan said. 'I'll stick to things that are on the earth.'

'Do be quiet!' Daft-Ingborg said. 'Do you think I'm so crazy that I'd go looking for things up in the sky? I just look for the ones that have fallen. I'm not stupid, you know.'

She opened her basket and Jan could see it was full of stars of many different kinds which she must have begged around the grand houses. There were stars made of tin and paper and glass, and Christmas tree decorations and sweets.

'They are real stars,' she said. 'They have fallen from Heaven. You're the only one who's been allowed to see them, and you can share some of them when you need to.'

'Thank you, Ingborg!' Jan said. 'When the time comes and I need stars, which may be quite soon, I shan't be asking you for them.'

Now, at last, she left, but it was a while before Jan went back to the threshing.

It was a sign, that's what it was. It wasn't that someone as crazy as Ingborg knew what was going on in Klara's life, but she was one of those people who could sense in the air when something remarkable was about to happen. She could see and hear things that right-minded folk would never even suspect.

Waiting

E very morning Boraeus, the engineer at Borg ironworks, used to take a turn down to the landing stage to meet the steamboat. There was nothing strange about that: he only had a short distance to walk through the fine park of spruce trees and there was always someone alighting from the boat with whom he could exchange a few words and gain some small relief from the monotony of country life.

There were several large, bare slabs of rock poking out of the ground just at the edge of the park, where the road began its steep descent to the landing stage, and people who had come a long distance would often sit down on them while they were waiting. There were always many people waiting at Borg Landing because it was impossible to be certain when the boat would come. It was rarely there before noon but, on the other hand, there was always a chance that it might arrive at the landing stage at eleven o'clock, and it wasn't completely unknown for it to be delayed until one or two o'clock. So cautious folk who arrived at ten o'clock might well find themselves sitting there the whole morning.

Boraeus the engineer had a good view along Lake Löven from his window at Borg. He could see when the steamboat appeared around the headlands and consequently he always arrived down at the landing at just the right time. So he never had to sit on the rocks and wait, and he usually gave no more than a passing glance at the people sitting there.

One summer, however, he couldn't help noticing a small man with a kind and gentle expression who sat there day after day. He would remain completely still and unconcerned until the steamboat appeared, when he would leap to his feet and his face would gleam with joy. He would then rush down the hill and take up a position right out at the end of the landing stage as if he was certain someone would arrive. But no one ever came for him and when the boat sailed he would still be standing there all alone as before.

The joy in his face was all gone now, and when he set off home he looked old and weary. Anyone watching him would be afraid he might not have the strength to climb the hill.

Boraeus did not know the man, but one beautiful sunny day when he saw him sitting there staring out over the lake, he struck up a conversation with him. He soon learnt that the man had a daughter who had left home but whose return was expected any day.

'Do you know for sure that she'll be coming today?' the engineer asked. 'I've seen you sitting here waiting for a couple of months. She must have misinformed you.'

'No, she certainly hasn't done that,' the man said in a gentle voice. 'She hasn't given me the wrong information, she hasn't.'

'But in Heaven's name,' the engineer said in a rather testy voice, for he was an irascible gentleman. 'What do you mean? You've been sitting here waiting day after day and she hasn't arrived. And you say she can't have given you the wrong information!'

'No,' the small man said, his kindly, clear eyes looking up at the engineer. 'She can't have done, because she hasn't given me any information at all.'

'Haven't you received a letter?' the engineer asked.

'No, we haven't had a letter since the first of October last year.'

'Why do you come down here then?' the engineer asked. 'You sit here doing nothing every morning. Do you have time to leave work like this?'

'No, I suppose it's bad of me,' the man said, smiling to himself, 'but it will all work out well in the end.'

'Can you really be so foolish as to hang around waiting for no reason at all?' the engineer exclaimed, quite enraged by this point. 'You ought to be in the madhouse!'

The man did not answer. He sat there quite unmoved, his

arms around his knees. A slight smile was still playing on his lips and, in fact, it seemed more and more triumphant with every passing moment.

Boraeus the engineer shrugged his shoulders and walked away. But when he was only halfway down the hill he changed his mind and turned back. The expression on his face was kindly. All the bitterness that usually shaded his stern features had gone. He held out his hand to the man.

'I just want to shake your hand,' he said. 'I believed I was the person in this parish who knew most about yearning, but now I see I have more than met my match.'

The Empress

The little girl from Skrolycka had been away for fully thirteen months without Jan betraying with a single word that he knew of the great good fortune that had befallen her. He was firmly resolved to remain silent until she herself returned. If Klara was unaware that he knew anything in advance, her pleasure at surprising him with her grandeur would be that much greater.

But in this world of ours the unexpected tends to happen more often than we expect. And so the day came when Jan had to spell out the situation without mincing his words. It wasn't for his own sake. He would have been quite happy to go round in his ragged clothes and let people believe he was no more than a poverty-stricken cottar for as long as necessary. No, it was for their little girl's sake that he was forced to reveal the great secret.

It was a day at the beginning of August and he had been down to the steamboat landing to wait for her. He found it impossible to resist going down there every day to see if she had come. She couldn't disapprove of that, could she?

The boat had just drawn alongside and he saw Klara wasn't there. He believed she would have finished everything by now and been able to return home but, no doubt, just as throughout the summer, something had turned up to prevent her coming. It wasn't easy to get away when you were involved in as many things as she was.

It was a great pity, though, that she hadn't come that day because unusually many of her old acquaintances were at the landing place. Karl Karlsson, the Riksdag man from Storvik was there, as was August Där Nol from Prästerud. Björn

Hindriksson's son-in-law was there, and even old Agrippa Prästberg happened to be there. Agrippa had harboured a grudge against the little girl ever since she'd tricked him about his spectacles. Jan couldn't deny what a pleasure it would have been if Klara had been on the boat that day and Prästberg had seen her in all her finery.

But since she wasn't there, the only thing for Jan to do was to go home. He was about to leave the landing stage when Grippa, as spiteful as he was old, stepped in front of him.

'Aha,' Grippa said, 'so you're down here after your daughter again today, are you?'

It's best not to bandy words with a man like Grippa and Jan stepped to the side in order to get past him.

'I'm not surprised you want to meet the sort of fine lady I hear she has become!' Grippa said.

August Där Nol came hurrying over to Grippa and tugged at his arm to make him keep quiet.

But Grippa wasn't about to give way.

'The whole parish knows,' he said, 'and it's about time her parents heard what's going on. Jan Andersson is a good man even if he did spoil his daughter. I can't put up with it any longer – seeing him sitting here week after week waiting for a - - -'

And here he used a word so vile about the little girl from Skrolycka that her father Jan could never bring himself to repeat it even in his thoughts.

But now that Agrippa Prästberg had hurled that word at him at the top of his voice in the hearing of all the people on the landing stage, everything that Jan had carried within him in silence for a whole year burst forth. He could no longer keep it hidden. His little girl would have to forgive him for betraying her.

He said what he had to say, without anger and without boasting. He waved it away with his hand and pursed his lips as though disdaining to answer.

'When the empress comes ...'

'The empress, what do you mean by that?' Grippa sneered, pretending to have heard nothing of the little girl's elevation.

But Jan from Skrolycka did not let himself be put off and continued as calmly as before.

'When Empress Klara of Portugallia is standing here on this landing stage with the golden crown on her head, when she is surrounded by seven kings carrying her train and there are seven lions lying tamely at her feet and seven and seventy captains walking before her with drawn swords in their hands, then, Prästberg, we shall see if you dare say to her what you have said to me today.'

After saying this he stood still for a moment to enjoy seeing how terrified they all were. Then he turned on his heel and departed, without any unseemly haste, of course.

As soon as he turned his back, an outcry broke out behind him. At first he paid no attention, but when he heard a loud thud he had to turn to look.

Old Grippa lay outstretched on the landing stage and August Där Nol was standing bent over him with clenched fists.

'You knew, didn't you, you wretch, that he couldn't bear to hear the truth,' August said. 'You have no heart, no heart at all!'

That was as much as Jan heard. Violence and fighting were against his nature and he carried on up the hill without becoming involved in the trouble.

But the strange thing was that once out of sight of all the people he was overwhelmed by an uncontrollable flood of tears. He had no explanation. They must surely have been tears of joy at finally being able to reveal his secret. He felt he had been given back his little girl.

The Emperor

On the first Sunday in September the Svartsjö congregation was given something to wonder at. They were indeed!

The Svartsjö church has a big, wide gallery that runs across the church above the nave. As long as anyone can remember, the gentry have sat in the front pew of the gallery, gentlemen to the right and wives and young ladies to the left.

All the places in the church were free to everyone, so others were not actually prohibited from sitting there, but it would never have occurred to a poor cottar to sit in that pew.

In the past Jan had always thought the people who sat up there were a grand and handsome sight to behold and even today he was not going to deny that the ironmaster from Duvnäs, the lieutenant from Lövdala and the engineer from Borg were fine-looking fellows. But they scarcely merited mention in the same breath as the magnificent sight the congregation now witnessed, for if there is one thing of which we can be certain it is that a seat in the gentry pew had never before been occupied by such a figure as a real emperor.

But there, occupying the most important place at the end of the pew, sat just such a grand figure. Both his hands were resting on a long cane with a large silver knob, on his head was a tall cap made of green leather, and two large stars – one seemed to be gold and the other silver – gleamed on his chest.

When the organ began playing, the emperor raised his voice and sang, for an emperor has the right to sing out loud and clear in church even if he is incapable of staying in tune. People are pleased to hear him anyway.

The gentlemen sitting beside him turned to look at him

time after time, but that was hardly to be wondered at as this was the first occasion they'd had such majesty among them.

He had to remove his cap, of course, because even an emperor has to do so in church, but he left it on as long as possible to allow people to feast their eyes on it.

Many of those sitting in the nave of the church that day turned their heads up to view the gallery and they paid more attention to him than to the sermon. They can be forgiven for that: once they had become accustomed to the presence of an emperor in their church, behaviour of that kind would pass.

They may well have been a little surprised that he had risen so high, but they ought to have realised that the father of an empress must himself be an emperor. Anything else would be unthinkable.

When the service was over and Jan came out to where the churchgoers were chatting, many people were on the point of approaching him, but before he had time to talk to anyone Cantor Svartling asked him to accompany him into the vestry.

When Jan and the cantor entered, the minister was sitting in a high armchair with his back to the door. He was talking to Karl Karlsson, the Riksdag man. It was possible to hear from the minister's voice that he was sorry about something – indeed, he was actually close to tears.

'That's two of the souls entrusted to my care that I have allowed to go to ruin,' he said.

Karl Karlsson tried to comfort him. 'You cannot possibly be blamed, minister, for the sin practised in the cities,' he said.

But the minister would not be comforted. Bent forward, he wept, his handsome young face in his hands. 'No, of course I can't,' he said. 'But what did I do to watch over the eighteen-year-old girl who was thrown unprotected out into the world? And what did I do to comfort the father who only had her to live for?'

'You haven't been long in this parish, minister,' the Riksdag man said. 'If there is to be any talk of responsibility, it should fall upon those of us who had knowledge of the situation. But who would have believed it could go so wrong? The young must be permitted to venture out into the world. We have all

– every one of us in the parish – been pushed out in a similar way and things have turned out well for most of us.'

'O God, if only I could speak to him!' the minister said. 'I only I could settle his wandering mind ...'

Cantor Svartling with Jan standing beside him cleared his throat and the minister turned round. He got to his feet at once and took Jan's hand in his own.

'Dear Jan!' he said.

The minister was tall, fair-haired and handsome. When he approached you with his fine voice and with his gentle blue eyes shining with compassion, he was not an easy man to resist. But in the present situation the only thing to do was to put him right immediately, which is precisely what Jan did.

'I am no longer Jan, dear minister, I am now Emperor Johannes of Portugallia, and I have nothing to say to anyone who is unwilling to use the proper form of address.'

With that Jan gave the minister a slight but imperial nod of farewell and put his cap on his head. He pushed open the door and departed, leaving the three men in the vestry looking more than a little astonished.

III.

The Imperial Song

On the forested slopes above Lobyn lay a section of the old country road that everyone had used in the old days. It was condemned as unfit now because it did nothing but snake up and down every possible hill and fell without ever having the sense to go round them. The small stretch that was left was so steep that it was never used by anyone driving a carriage or cart, though the occasional walker would struggle up and down it because it offered a good short cut.

But it was still the official width of a highway of the realm, and it was still covered with good yellow gravel, better now, in fact, than before since there were no wheel ruts, mud or dust. And the plants that flower along roadsides still bloomed there – chervil and bitter vetch and buttercups in serried ranks. The ditches had fallen in, however, and become overgrown, allowing a long row of spruce trees to escape from the forest. They were just young trees, all the same height and with branches from root to top, and they were packed as close together as a manor house hedge. Not a single one of them had dried out or turned brown. Their tops showed young, light-green shoots and in the beautiful days of summer when the sun shone down from a clear sky they were filled with the humming of bumble bees.

On his way home from church on the Sunday he first revealed himself in his imperial finery, Jan decided to take the old road. It was a hot and sunny day and as he walked up the hill he heard the music of the spruce trees so loud that he was filled with amazement. He couldn't remember ever having heard trees singing like that, and the thought occurred to him that he should try to find out why it all sounded so loud on that day in particular. Being in no hurry, he sat down on the gravel of the road among the trees, laid his cane beside him, took off his cap to wipe the sweat from his brow and then, hands folded, sat quietly and listened.

The air was utterly still and there was no breeze to set all the small instruments in motion. The only explanation seemed to be that the spruce trees were making music to show how happy they were to be young and healthy, to be left to themselves here along the old deserted road, to have so many years to look forward to before anyone thought of chopping them down.

But if that was the case it still failed to explain why the trees were making music so forcefully on this particular day. After all, they could rejoice in all those good gifts on any fine summer's day without needing to make extra music.

Jan sat silently in the middle of the road and listened.

The murmur of the trees was beautiful even though the same note went on and on endlessly. There was no element of melody or rhythm.

It was so lovely and sweet on the wooded hillside that it was little wonder the trees felt happy and joyful. What was truly remarkable was that the spruce trees could not possibly have made better music than they were making. He looked at their small twigs on which every needle was fine and green and well-formed and in its proper place. He inhaled the scent of resin they exuded. None of the plants in the meadow or flowers in the garden smelled that good. He noticed their half-grown cones, on which the scales were skilfully arranged to protect the seeds.

These trees understood everything, so surely they could play and sing in a way that people could understand?

But the trees continued sounding the same continuous note and as he sat listening to them Jan grew sleepy. Stretching out on this clean gravel road and taking a nap didn't seem such a bad idea.

But wait! What's this? The moment he laid his head on the ground and closed his eyes the trees started something new. Now there was a tempo, now there was a melody.

Everything so far had been no more than a prelude of the kind played in church before a hymn is sung, but now it was accompanied by words – words he could understand.

So this was it, this was what he had sensed the whole time although he had hesitated to express it even in his thoughts. But the trees knew everything that had happened, they really did, and it was for him they had played so loudly when he arrived here.

Now they thought he was asleep, they were singing about him, there was no mistaking it. It seemed that they didn't want him to hear them celebrating him.

What a song it was! What a melody! He lay there and kept his eyes closed, which allowed him to hear so much better. There wasn't a sound that escaped him.

After the first verses had been sung there came an intermezzo without words, and it was magnificent.

What music! Now it was not just the young trees that lined the old road, now the whole forest was joining in. There were organs and drums and trumpets. There were small thrush flutes and chaffinch pipes, becks and kelpies, chiming bluebells and drumming woodpeckers.

He had never heard anything so wonderful, and he had never listened to music in that way. It entered his ears and stayed, never to be forgotten.

When the singing came to an end and the forest fell silent once more, he rose as if from a dream and, so as not to forget it, immediately began singing the emperor's song the forest had sung him.

This is the heartfelt happiness
Of the father of the Empress.

That was followed by a refrain, which he had been unable to pick out properly, but he sang it anyway, more or less as he thought it had sounded.

As the newspapers all have it.
Austria, Portugal,

Metz, Japan, as it was.
Boom, boom, boom and roll
Boom, boom.

His cap a golden crown,
His sword a golden gun.
As the newspapers all have it.
Austria, Portugal,
Metz, Japan, as it was.
Boom, boom, boom and roll
Boom, boom.

Golden apples float and bob
Like turnips in his pot.
As the newspapers all have it.
Austria, Portugal,
Metz, Japan, as it was.
Boom, boom, boom and roll
Boom, boom.

When he leaves his cabin low
All the gentlewomen bow.
As the newspapers all have it.
Austria, Portugal,
Metz, Japan, as it was.
Boom, boom, boom and roll
Boom, boom.

When he marches through the wood
Trees and leaves all feel so good.
As the newspapers all have it.
Austria, Portugal,
Metz, Japan, as it was.
Boom, boom, boom and roll
Boom, boom.

It was precisely this 'boom, boom' that had sounded more
magnificent than all the rest. He thumped his cane hard on

the ground with every 'boom' and made his voice as deep and strong as possible.

He sang the song and then he sang it time after time so that it echoed through the forest. There was something so wonderful about it that he did not weary of singing it over and over again.

But, then, the way in which the song had come into being was so unusual. The fact that for the only time in his life a melody had lodged firmly in his mind must surely be a sign of how special it was.

The Seventeenth of August

The first time Jan from Skrolycka went to Lövdala Manor on the seventeenth of August his visit had not been as respectable as he might have wished. He had not been back since, not once, even though he'd heard people say that the Lövdala celebrations were becoming more enjoyable and impressive from one year to the next.

But now, of course, following the elevation of his little girl, everything had changed. He believed that Lieutenant Liljekrona would be quite mortified if a figure as important as Emperor Johannes of Portugallia failed to do him the honour of wishing him well on his birthday.

Jan donned his imperial finery and set off, making sure, however, that he did not arrive among the first guests. Since he was emperor, it was appropriate for him to allow the many guests to settle in and the festivities to be under way before he made his entrance.

On his previous visit he had not dared go beyond the garden and the gravel drive in front of the house, and he had not gone up to the lieutenant and expressed his good wishes. But such unmannerly behaviour was now out of the question and he made his way directly to the large arbour to the left of the terrace at the front of the house, which was where the lieutenant was sitting among a crowd of gentlemen from Svartsjö and further afield. There he took him by the hand and wished him a happy birthday and many more to come!

'Aha, Jan, I see you are out and about,' Lieutenant Liljekrona said, sounding a little surprised. He had clearly not been expecting to be the recipient of such an honour and that, no doubt, was why he had forgotten his manners and called Jan by his old name.

Jan knew that a well-mannered fellow like the lieutenant would not have meant any harm by doing so, which was why he corrected him gently.

'We won't be over particular today, lieutenant, since it's your birthday,' Jan said. 'But properly speaking it should be Johannes of Portugallia.'

He said these words in as mild a voice as possible, in spite of which the other gentlemen began laughing at the lieutenant for having behaved so foolishly. Vexation of this kind on the lieutenant's birthday was the last thing Jan had wanted to cause and so he turned to the gentlemen in an attempt to change the subject.

'Good day, good day, my dear generals, bishops and governors!' he said, raising his cap with a grand imperial gesture. It was his intention to go round the circle and shake them all by the hand, as one does on joining a party.

Sitting closest to the lieutenant was a fat little man wearing a white waistcoat. He had gold on his collar and a sword at his side. When Jan approached him, the man offered him two fingers rather than the whole of his hand.

It is possible that he meant nothing by it, but a man like Emperor Johannes knows only too well the importance of standing on one's dignity.

'You're very welcome to give me your whole hand, my dear bishop and county governor,' Jan said in the friendliest of voices since he had no desire to disrupt the happiness of the great day.

But believe it or not, the man turned up his nose!

'A moment ago I heard that you were put out when Liljekrona called you by name,' he said. 'And now I'm wondering how you can have the cheek to speak to me in such a familiar fashion. Can't you see these?' he asked, pointing to three pitifully small stars on his coat.

Well, when words like that are uttered, it is time to put humility aside. Jan threw his coat open to reveal his waistcoat, which was completely covered with a dazzling array of big 'medallions', both gold and silver. He normally kept his coat buttoned over them since they were delicate and might easily fade or be damaged. And since people are often strangely embarrassed in the company of great men, he didn't want to intimidate them by showing off his splendour unnecessarily. But now it had to be done.

'You there, take a look at this!' Jan said. 'Huh, huh, huh! This is what you need if you want to boast. Three miserable stars – what do you call that?'

This, as you can imagine, made the man show more respect, helped, no doubt, by all those who knew about the empress and the empire beginning to laugh uproariously at him.

'Lord in Heaven!' the man said, rising to his feet and bowing. 'I am obviously face to face with real royalty! And, what's more, he has a tongue in his head.'

That is how things go when you know how to deal with people. Once that was cleared up, no one was keener to converse with the ruler of Portugallia than the man who had initially been so touchy as to offer only two fingers to an emperor who proffered him a whole hand.

It seems unnecessary to report that, subsequently, none of the men sitting in the arbour declined to greet the emperor in a suitable manner. Once that first confusion and embarrassment had been overcome and the assembled gentlemen had begun to realise that Jan, emperor though he may be, was not a difficult man to get on with, they became as eager as everyone else to hear his account of his little girl's elevation and of her imminent return to her home parish. In the end they proved so friendly that he sang them the song he had learnt in the forest. In this he was perhaps lowering himself rather more than was proper, but since they were enjoying every word he said, he couldn't deny them the pleasure of hearing his song.

When he raised his voice to sing it caused considerable excitement. His audience, which had only consisted of the old gentlemen, was now joined by the ageing countesses and generals' wives who had been drinking tea and eating sweets on the sofa in the drawing room. And they, in turn, were joined by the young barons and maids of honour who had been dancing in the ballroom but now came rushing to listen. They formed a close circle around him and all eyes were fixed on him, which is as it should be when you are an emperor.

They had never heard anything like his song before, of course, and no sooner had he finished singing than they wanted him to start again. They had to press him for some time – after all, an emperor shouldn't be too amenable – but they wouldn't give up until he did what they wanted. When he reached the refrain they joined in, and when it came to the 'boom, boom boom' the young barons stamped on the ground and the maids of honour clapped in time.

It really was a remarkable song. Singing it now with so many beautifully dressed people joining in and so many pretty young girls throwing friendly glances at him and so many dashing young gentlemen shouting hurrah after every verse, he began to feel as giddy as if he'd been dancing. He felt he was being taken under the arms and raised high in the air.

He did not lose consciousness and he remained aware he was still on earth, but at the same time he felt how sweet it was to rise so high above all the others. On one side it was honour raising him up, and on the other glory. They carried him on strong wings and placed him on an imperial throne far away among the red clouds of evening.

Only one thing was missing. If only the great empress, little Klara Goldie from Skrolycka could have been there too!

No sooner had that thought crossed his mind than a shimmer of red spread over the garden. When he looked more closely he saw it was emanating from a young girl in red who had come out of the house and was standing on the terrace.

She was tall and she had a mass of golden hair. The way she was standing made it impossible for him to see her face, but it couldn't be anyone but Klara.

And now he understood why he had been feeling so blissfully happy that evening. It had been a premonition that she was close.

He broke off in the middle of the song, elbowed aside the people in his way and ran towards the manor house.

When he reached the bottom of the steps he had to stop.

His heart was beating so violently that his chest was on the point of bursting.

Eventually enough strength returned to allow him to move forward again and he ascended slowly step by step. At last he reached the terrace, spread his arms wide and whispered her name.

The young girl turned round. It was not Klara, but a stranger who was looking at him in astonishment.

He could not say a word and the tears ran down his face. He could not hold them back. He went down the steps, turned his back on all the joy and splendour and set off up the avenue.

People called to him, called to him to come back and sing to them, but he didn't hear them. As soon as he could he hurried into the forest where he could hide himself and his sorrow.

Jan and Kattrinna

J an at Skrolycka had never before had so much to think
about as he had now that he was emperor.

In the first place, since greatness had been bestowed
upon him, he knew he constantly needed to be on his
guard against allowing pride to enter his life. He must bear in
mind that we humans are all made of the same stuff, that we
are all descendants of the same ancestral couple, that we are
all weak and sinful and that, essentially, none of us has any
claim to be superior to the rest.

Throughout his life it had saddened him to see people
trying to lord it over their fellows and he did not want to
behave in that way. But he could not help noticing that it
wasn't easy to remain properly humble when you have been
raised so high that you have no equals in the parish.

What worried him most, of course, was that he might do or
say something that would make his old friends feel overlooked
and forgotten as they went about their daily tasks and
labours. Almost certainly the best thing to do when attending
celebrations and festivities in the district, as was now his
duty, was to avoid telling people what had happened to him.
He must not accuse them of envy – perish the thought! – but
he ought not force them to make comparisons.

Nor should he demand that men like Börje and the net
maker call him emperor. Old friends like that must be allowed
to call him Jan as they had always done. It would never occur
to them to do anything different anyway.

But the person he had to give most consideration to was,
of course, his wife, the old woman with whom he shared a
home. It would have been a great relief, and a joy, if she too

had received the call to greatness, but it hadn't happened and she remained as before. Perhaps that was inevitable. Klara must have realised that it was impossible to make an empress of Kattrinna. It was quite impossible to imagine her wearing a golden tiara to church. She would almost certainly prefer to stay at home rather than be seen with anything other than her black silk scarf on her head.

Kattrinna said bluntly that she did not want to hear any talk of Klara becoming an empress and, when all was said and done, it was probably best to do as she wanted in that matter.

When he went down to the landing stage every morning he was surrounded by people waiting for the boat and they did not fail to address him as emperor at every opportunity. So it's not hard to understand how difficult it was for him to put aside his majesty when he stepped over the threshold of his own home. And it has to be said that he found carrying firewood and water for Kattrinna a trying business while she was still addressing him as if he had gone down in the world rather than up.

If Kattrinna had confined herself to that, it would have been quite acceptable, but she also complained because he was no longer willing to go out and work as a day labourer. When she started on that topic, however, he turned a deaf ear. He knew – just knew – that the Empress of Portugallia was going to send him so much money that he would never again have to don his work clothes. Giving in to Kattrinna on that matter would have been nothing short of an impertinence to the empress.

One afternoon at the end of August Jan was sitting on the rock outside the front door smoking his stubby pipe when he caught a glimpse of bright dresses and heard young voices coming from the forest.

Kattrinna had gone down to the birch grove to cut twigs for a broom, but before she went she had told him that from now on she would have to go and dig ditches at Falla Farm. He could stay at home and cook and patch the clothes since working for other people was now beneath him. He hadn't said a word in response – just listening to her was hard enough – and he was now more than happy to have an opportunity to think about other things. He hurried indoors to fetch his imperial cap and cane and managed to reach the gate just as the young girls were passing.

There were no fewer than five of them and among them were the three young ladies from Lövdala Manor. The other two were strangers, who had presumably come visiting.

Jan opened the gate wide and walked towards them.

'Good day, my dear maids of honour!' he said, sweeping his cap so low it almost touched the ground.

They came to a sudden halt and looked rather shy at first, but he quickly helped them over their initial embarrassment.

What followed was 'good day' and 'our dear emperor' and it was soon very obvious that it gave them real pleasure to see him again.

Unlike Kattrinna and the other people from Askedalarna, these young gentlewomen had no objection at all to hearing about the empress, and without further ado they asked him how she was and whether she was expected home soon.

They also wondered whether they might go into the cottage to see what it was like inside. There was no reason to deny them, for Kattrinna always kept things so clean and tidy that anyone was welcome to call at any time.

When the young ladies from the manor were inside, there can be no doubt they were surprised that a great empress had grown up in such a small place. It may have suited her before, they said, when she was used to it, but what would it be like when she returned? Was she going to come and live with her parents or would she be returning to Portugallia?

Jan had actually wondered about the same thing. He had, of course, realised that Klara could not stay in Askedalarna when she had a whole empire to rule over.

'I've no doubt the empress will be going back to Portugallia,' he said.

'And presumably you will be accompanying her?' one of the young ladies asked.

In his heart Jan would have preferred her not to ask that question and at first he did not answer. But the young girl wouldn't drop the subject.

'Is it because you don't know what will happen?' she said.

Oh, but he did know. What he didn't know was how people would take his decision. They might think it wasn't the way an emperor should behave.

'I shall almost certainly stay at home, I shall,' he said. 'It wouldn't be right to leave Kattrinna.'

'So Kattrinna won't be going, then?'

'No, there's no hope of convincing Kattrinna to leave the cottage. And I shall be staying with her – for better or for worse, as we promised when we married.'

'Yes, I do understand that's a promise you can't go back on,' one of the young ladies said. She was the one who asked the most questions.

'Did you hear that, everyone?' she said. 'Jan will not leave his wife, not even for all the splendours of Portugallia.'

They were so happy to hear this that they patted his shoulder and said he was doing the right thing. It was a good sign, they said. It wasn't the end of kind old Jan Andersson from Skrolycka yet.

He didn't really understand what they meant; presumably they were happy he would be staying in the parish.

They said goodbye and departed. They were walking over to Duvnäs for a party.

No sooner had they gone than Kattrinna came in! She must have been waiting outside the door rather than coming in while the visitors were there. How long she had been there and how much of the conversation she had heard is impossible to say.

She was, however, looking a good deal milder and gentler than she had done for a long time.

'You're a real fool,' she said, 'and I wonder what other women would have to say if they had a husband like you. But for all that, it's good that you don't want to leave me.'

The Funeral

Jan Andersson at Skrolycka had neither been informed about nor invited to attend the funeral of Björn Hindriksson at Lobyn. No word had come, but it may be that the family of the deceased was uncertain as to whether he considered himself related to them now that he had risen to a position of such honour and magnificence.

They may have thought that things would be difficult to organise if a man of such stature were to attend the funeral. Björn Hindriksson's closest relatives would naturally want to ride at the front of the cortège, but rightfully speaking there should be a place there for Jan since he was an emperor.

They weren't to know, of course, that he did not set much store by things that others considered important. It never occurred to him, for instance, to stand in the way of people who enjoyed occupying the front seats at parties.

So, in order not to cause difficulties, he did not go to the deceased's farm in the morning before the cortège set off and went instead straight to the church. Only when the bells were rung and the long procession was forming up outside the church did he step forward and take his place among the relatives.

The people in the funeral procession looked more than a little taken aback at his presence, but by now he was quite used to people being surprised by his willingness to come down to their level. He had no doubt they would have wanted to make space for him at the front, but there wasn't time as the procession was already moving towards the graveyard.

When the burial was over and he accompanied the funeral party back to the church and sat in the same pew as them, once again they looked rather embarrassed, but since the opening hymn was starting they didn't have time to comment on the fact he had moved down from his grand seat up on the balcony.

At the end of the service, when all the carriages for the mourners were drawn up outside the church, Jan went and sat on the big, open-sided wagon which had carried the coffin on the way to the church. He knew that particular wagon would be returning empty and so he would not be taking anyone else's seat. Björn Hindriksson's daughter and son-in-law walked past several times and looked at him sitting there. It may have been because they were concerned that they couldn't invite him to ride in one of the foremost carriages, but he had no wish for people to be moved around for his sake. He was who he was in any case.

As they moved away from the church he could not help remembering the time he and little Klara had come here to visit their rich relations. Everything was quite different now, of course. Who was powerful and respected now? Who brought honour on the others by paying a visit?

As the mourners arrived back at the farm they were led into the big living room on the lower floor, where they took off their coats. Then Björn Hindriksson's neighbours, who had been asked to act as hosts, came in and invited the more prominent of the guests to come to the upper floor where a table was laid for a meal. Choosing who was to go upstairs was a great responsibility since, at such a large funeral, it would be impossible to seat all the guests at the dinner table at the same time and there would have to be several sittings. Many of the people there, however, would have considered it so insulting not to have been selected for the first sitting that they would never have forgiven the slight.

Now, in the case of Jan, a man of imperial status, there were many situations in which he was willing to be accommodating, but he felt compelled to stand firm on the issue of being selected for the first sitting. Failure to do so might lead people to think he was uncertain about his rights of precedence.

There was, of course, no danger of that, even though he

wasn't among the very first to be invited upstairs. After all, it was so self-evident that he should dine at the same time as the minister and the gentry that he had no reason to be concerned.

He sat silent and alone on a bench, for no one here came up to him wanting to talk about the empress. He felt a little despondent, of that there was no doubt. Kattrinna had said to him as he was leaving home that he ought not go to this funeral because the people on the farm were of such a superior family that they didn't bow down to kings or to emperors. It was looking as if she'd been right. Old farming families that have worked the same farm since God created the earth consider themselves a cut above everyone else, however grand.

Selecting and collecting those who were to join the first sitting could not be hurried. The host and hostess spent a long time going round picking out the most worthy guests, but they did not approach Jan.

He was sitting beside a couple of unmarried women who had no hope at all of being chosen this early. They were enjoying a quiet chat and they mentioned what a good thing it was that Linnart Björnsson, Björn Hindriksson's son, had managed to come home in time to be reconciled with his father.

It wasn't that there had been any great enmity between them. What had happened was that some thirty years before, when Linnart was in his early twenties, he had asked his father to let him take over the farm or, if not, to agree to some other arrangement whereby Linnart could be his own man. But Björn had said no to both those things: he wanted his son to stay at home as before and not take over the farm until his father had been laid to rest.

At that point the son is thought to have said: 'I don't want to stay here and be just a farmhand on your farm even though you are my father. I'd rather go out into the world and get a farm of my own, for I want to be as much of a man as you are. If I stay we'll soon be at loggerheads.'

'Which may well happen anyway if you go off on your own,'

Björn Hindriksson is supposed to have answered.

The son had then moved up to the great forests north and east of Lake Duvsjön, settled out there in the wilds, cleared land and made a farm. His farm was in the parish of Bro and he never showed his face back in Svartsjö. His parents had not seen him for thirty years, but eight days ago he had turned up at home just when old Björn was lying on his deathbed.

Jan from Skrolycka was happy to hear this good news. When Kattrinna had come home from church the previous Sunday with the news that Björn Hindriksson was not long for this world, Jan immediately asked after the son and wondered whether he had been sent for. He had not. Kattrinna had heard that Björn Hindriksson's wife had begged and pleaded to be allowed to send a message, but she had been strictly forbidden to do so. The old man had said that he wanted peace and quiet on his deathbed.

Jan had not been satisfied with this. He couldn't stop thinking about Linnart Björnsson living up there in the forest and not knowing, so he, Jan, had decided to go against old Björn's wishes and take the news up to his son.

He had not heard what happened after that until he came to the funeral, and he was so busy listening to the story the two women had to tell that he completely forgot to think about both the first and the second sittings of the meal.

It seems that when the son arrived home he and his father were very happy to see one another. They really were. The old man had laughed and looked at his son's clothes.

'You've come in your work clothes,' he said.

'Yes, I know I should have dressed up since it's Sunday,' Linnart had answered, 'but we've had so much rain up our way this summer that I was going to bring in some of the oats even though it's Sunday afternoon.'

'Did you manage to get some in?' the old man asked.

'I managed to load up a wagon, but I left it out on the field when I heard the message. I set off straightaway without bothering to change my clothes.'

'Who was it who brought you the message?' his father asked after a while.

'A fellow I've never seen before,' his son answered. 'I didn't think to ask who he was – he actually looked like a little old beggar.'

'Well, you find out who he is and thank him from me,' old Björn was supposed to have said very emphatically. 'You must show him respect wherever you meet him. He meant well by us.'

And that's how things remained between them, calm and good, right to the end. They were so happy to be reconciled that it was almost as if death had brought them joy rather than sorrow.

Jan was rather put out when he heard that Linnart Björnsson had described him as a beggar. But then he realised it was because he had not been wearing his cap or carrying his imperial cane up in the wilds.

This reminded him of his present concerns. He had, he thought, undoubtedly been waiting long enough now. He really should have been called upstairs already, otherwise it would be too late. Things weren't being done properly.

He stood up, strode resolutely across the room and hall, climbed the stairs and opened the door of the main room on the upper floor.

He saw at once that the meal was in full swing, every seat at the big horseshoe table was taken and the first course was already being served. It was obvious they had not intended to include him among the prominent people. There was the minister, there was the cantor, there was the lieutenant from Lövdala Manor along with his wife. All those who should be there were there – apart from him.

No sooner was he in through the door than one of the young girls serving the food hurried over to him.

'What are you doing here, Jan?' she said in a low voice. 'Downstairs with you, now!'

'But my dear serving girl!' Jan said. 'Emperor Johannes of Portugallia should be at the first sitting.'

'Quiet! Enough now, Jan!' the girl said. 'This is not the day for you to come out with all your silly notions. Go down now and you'll be fed when it's your turn.'

The fact is that Jan had more respect for this house than for any other house in the parish, which was why he thought it so important to be received here in a manner appropriate to his status. As he stood in the doorway, cap in hand, he was overwhelmed by a sudden and strange sense of dejection. He felt all his imperial majesty falling away.

But then, in the middle of this dreadful predicament, he heard Linnart Björnsson over at the table suddenly utter an exclamation.

'That's the fellow, that one over there, who came to me last Sunday with the message that Father was ill!' he said.

'What's that?' his mother said. 'Are you sure?'

'I am! It couldn't be anyone else. I saw him earlier today but didn't recognise him because he was so strangely dressed. But now I can see that it's him.'

'Well if it's him, he shouldn't be standing over by the door like a beggar,' the old woman said. 'We must make a space for him here at the table. We owe him our gratitude and our respect because it's thanks to him that old Björn had an easy death, which is the only consolation I have in my grief at losing such a man.'

And so they made room, although it had already seemed a tight squeeze. Jan was given a seat on the inside of the horseshoe immediately opposite the minister. It could not have been better.

He was a little confused at first because he could not understand why they were making such a fuss of him just because he'd run a dozen miles through the forest to take news to Linnart Björnsson. But eventually he saw how it all hung together. It was, of course, the emperor they wanted to honour, and they were doing it this way, perhaps, so that no one would feel left out.

Anyway, no other explanation was given. And he actually had been kind and obliging and helpful every day of his life, although he had never been honoured and celebrated for it.

The Dying Heart

When Boraeus the engineer at Borg took his short daily walk down to the steamboat landing, it was impossible for him not to be aware of the gathering of people who constantly clustered around the little fellow from Skrolycka these days. He no longer had to sit alone, driving away the tedium with silent dreams, as he had done before. Instead, everyone waiting for the steamer came up to him to hear what was to happen when the empress returned home, especially when she came ashore here at Borg Landing. Every time the engineer walked past he heard of the golden tiara the empress would be wearing in her hair and of the golden flowers that would bloom on trees and bushes the moment she set foot on land.

One morning well into October, about three months after the day Jan first announced the news of Klara's elevation right here at Borg Landing, the engineer noticed that an unusually large crowd was gathered around him. Boraeus had intended to walk past with his usual short greeting, but he changed his mind and stopped to find out what was going on.

At first glance he was unable to see anything remarkable. Jan was sitting on the waiting rocks as he usually did, and his expression was very dignified and solemn. A big woman was sitting beside him and she was talking so eagerly and fast that the words were more or less tumbling from her mouth. When she finished saying what she wanted to say, she shook her head, screwed up her eyes and bent so far forward that her face was right down at ground level.

The engineer immediately recognised Daft-Ingborg of course, though initially he found it completely impossible to understand what she was saying. He had to ask one of the bystanders what it was all about.

'She's begging him to allow her to go to Portugallia with the empress when she returns there,' the bystander said. 'She's been on at him about it for a long time, but he won't give her a promise.'

The engineer had no trouble following the conversation after that, but he wasn't happy at what he heard. The furrow between his eyebrows grew red and deep as he listened.

Here was the only person in the world apart from Jan himself who believed in the wonders of Portugallia and she was being denied the chance to go there! The poor creature knew it was a land in which there was no hunger and no poverty, no coarse people who mocked an unfortunate, no children who followed lonely, helpless travellers for mile after mile throwing stones at them. Perpetual peace and good harvests were the rule there, and that is where she wished to be taken, away from the misery of her poor life. She begged and she wept and used all her powers of persuasion, but no and no again was the only answer she received.

And the man who was deaf to all her prayers was one who had spent the whole of the last year in longing and in sorrow. It's possible he would not have refused her a few months before, when there was still life in his heart, but now, now, in his time of success, it was as if that heart had turned to stone.

Even his outward appearance showed the great change he had undergone. His cheeks were plump, he had a double chin, and there was a thick, dark moustache on his upper lip. His eyes bulged slightly and his gaze had become fixed and staring. The engineer actually wondered whether his nose had grown larger and more aristocratic in shape. His hair seemed to have fallen out, as not a single strand was poking out under his leather cap.

The engineer had been watching Jan ever since their first conversation the summer before. It was no longer his great longing that drove Jan down to the landing stage and he scarcely even looked at the steamer these days. He only went there to meet people prepared to play along with his mad ideas and call him emperor in order to hear him sing his song and recount his fantasies.

But what was there to be angry about? After all, the fellow was a madman.

Perhaps the anger arose because there had been no need for his madness to have taken such a firm hold? It occurred to the engineer that if someone had firmly and mercilessly dragged him down from his imperial throne right at the start, he might have been saved.

The engineer gave Jan a searching look. Jan's expression was gracious and regretful, but he was not to be moved.

It was clear that this wonderful country Portugallia would only be peopled by princes and generals, finely dressed people and no one else. And Daft-Ingborg in her cotton scarf and home-knitted cardigan would have looked out of place there. 'But, God Almighty! Really!' the engineer thought.

It looked as if he felt like teaching Jan the lesson he needed, but then he shrugged his shoulders. He was not the right man to do it and would only have made things worse.

He walked silently away from the group of people and down to the landing stage. The steamer was just coming into sight around the nearest headland.

Dethroned

Once, long before he married Anna, the daughter of Farmer Erik at Falla Farm, Lars Gunnarsson had happened to attend an auction.

The people whose goods were being auctioned were poor. There did not appear to be much that buyers fancied and the auction was going unusually badly. The sellers had a right to expect better since the auctioneer was Jöns from Kisterud, who was such a comedian that people often went to auctions just to listen to him. But in spite of Jöns coming out with all his usual witticisms, he was finding it impossible to get the bidding going. In the end the only solution he could think of was to put down his gavel and say he was so hoarse it was impossible for him to continue.

'You'll have to find someone else to do the calling,' he said to Karl Karlsson, the Riksdag man, who was responsible for the auction. 'I've yelled myself so hoarse at these stone dummies that I'll have to go home and keep quiet for a couple of weeks to get my voice back.'

It was a serious matter for Karl Karlsson to be left without an auctioneer when most of the lots were still unsold, and he made several attempts to persuade Jöns to continue, but it was quite clear he would not do so. He didn't want to lose his good reputation by running a poor auction, but he was so hoarse that he couldn't even whisper the words. The only thing that emerged was a hissing noise.

'Is there anyone here who can call for bids for a while so that Jöns can take a break?' Karl Karlsson asked.

He was surveying the crowd without much hope of finding a helper, when Lars Gunnarsson pushed his way to the front and said he was willing to try. He looked so young in those days that Karl Karlsson just laughed at him and said he didn't have any use for boys who hadn't even been confirmed. Lars answered that he'd already done his military service, and he was so keen to try his hand with the gavel that Karl Karlsson agreed.

'Oh well, I suppose we can let you try,' he said. 'It can't get any worse than it already is.'

Lars stepped up and took Jöns's place. He picked up the next lot, which was a small butter tub, but then he hesitated and just stood looking at it. He turned it this way and that, tapped the bottom and the sides, looked surprised at being unable to find any fault with it, and then called for bids in a sad voice, as if he was unhappy to be forced to sell such a treasure.

It was obvious he would prefer there to be no bids. He believed it would be better for the seller if no one recognised how excellent this butter tub was so that the old owner could hang on to it.

Then, as one bid followed another, you could see how painful he was finding it. It was bearable when the bids were so low that he didn't need to listen to them, but as they rose higher and higher his whole face twisted in misery. He obviously considered it to be a major sacrifice when he was finally forced to bring down the gavel on the smelly old butter tub.

Then he moved on to buckets, pails and laundry tubs. Lars Gunnarsson was fairly content to sell the older items and did so without too many sighs. But when it came to newer things, he actually didn't want to auction them off. 'They are too good,' he said to the man who owned them. 'They've been used so little you could sell them as new at the market.'

The people at the auction had no idea how it happened but they found themselves bidding more and more enthusiastically. Lars Gunnarsson looked so anxious every time he called for a bid that he certainly couldn't be the reason they were bidding. Somehow or other, they had come to recognise that what he was auctioning had real value and they realised that this and that was needed back at home.

Money had begun to change hands and they weren't just buying for fun as they did when Jöns was the auctioneer.

After this demonstration of skill Lars Gunnarsson found himself in constant demand as auctioneer. When he took over the gavel the auctions weren't as much fun as in the past, but no one else had his ability to convince people that they were really longing to own some useless piece of old rubbish, or to seduce a couple of bigwigs into bidding against one another for things they had no use for, but just wanted to show they had money to spend.

At the auctions he ran, Lars Gunnarsson would normally sell every single lot. There was only one occasion when things looked to be going badly and that was the auction after the death of Sven Österberg at Storstuga in Bergvik. The lots to be auctioned were very fine, plenty of people had turned up, and even though it was well into autumn, the weather was so good that the auction could be held in the open air. But despite all this Lars was having no success. He couldn't get people interested in the lots and couldn't get them to bid. It looked as if the day would be no better for him than it had been for Jöns from Kisterud the time Lars had taken over from him.

But Lars had no intention of handing his office over to someone else and so he tried to work out what it was that was distracting people to the extent that they didn't want to buy anything. And it didn't take him very long to discover the reason.

Lars had climbed up on a table so everyone could see what he was auctioning, and from that vantage point he could see the new emperor, who lived in the cottage near Falla and had worked as a day labourer on the farm all his life. The emperor was moving around in the crowd and Lars saw him greeting people to right and left with gracious smiles while allowing them to study his smart cane and his stars. A long line of children and young people followed at his heels, and even old people were not above having a word with him. So, given the presence of a man of such stature making himself the focus of attention, it was hardly surprising that the auction was not going well.

Initially Lars did not interrupt the auction, but he followed Jan with his eyes until he had worked his way to the front and was close to the auctioneer. There was very little chance of Johannes of Portugallia staying in the background: he was shaking hands with everyone he knew, exchanging a few friendly words here and there and moving on until he was right at the front of the circle.

At the very moment Jan reached that point, Lars Gunnarsson leapt down from the table, rushed at Jan, snatched both the leather cap and the imperial cane and was back up on the table before Jan had time to think of resisting.

Jan shouted out loud and tried to clamber up on the table to retrieve his stolen treasures, but Lars swung at him with the cane and forced him to retreat. Meanwhile a murmur of displeasure rose from the crowd, but Lars did not allow that to deter him.

'I realise you are all astonished at my behaviour,' he shouted in his powerful auctioneer's voice that could be heard across the whole farm. 'But this cap and this cane belong to us at Falla Farm. My father-in-law Erik Ersa owned them and he inherited them from the old farmer who had the farm before him. These items have always been held in great esteem in our home and I cannot bear to see a fool going around wearing them. I can't say how he came by them, but one thing I know is that, as from now, he will not be allowed to wander around dressed in things that belong to us.'

Jan had calmed down quickly and while Lars was making his speech he stood with his arms crossed and an expression on his face that suggested indifference to anything Lars might say. As soon as Lars had finished, Jan turned to those present with an authoritative gesture and said:

'Now, gentlemen of my court, would you kindly restore my possessions to me?'

But not a single soul moved to help him and, even worse, some people actually laughed at him. They had all gone over to Lars's side.

One person and one alone felt sorry for him. He heard a woman's voice in the crowd shout to the auctioneer: 'Come along, Lars, let him have his emperor's finery back! You don't have any use for the cane or for the cap.'

'I'll give him one of my own caps when I get home,' Lars said. 'But his days of wandering around making a mockery of these family heirlooms are over.'

The crowd broke into loud laughter on hearing this and Jan was so confused that he stood rooted to the spot and stared all round. He turned from one person to another and couldn't get over his surprise. Dear heavens! Wasn't there anyone among all these people who had been praising and honouring him who would help in his hour of need? But no one moved. He saw that he meant nothing to them and that they weren't willing to do anything for him. He was so frightened that every vestige of imperial majesty disappeared and he looked like a child about to burst into tears because he has lost his toys.

Lars Gunnarsson turned to the large pile of goods alongside him and wanted to get the auction going again. Jan, however, tried to sort matters out for himself. Lamenting loudly, he went up to the table on which Lars was standing, bent down suddenly and tried to tip it over.

But he failed to catch Lars off guard. Lars lashed out with the imperial cane again and struck Jan's back so hard that he retreated.

'Oh no you don't,' Lars said. 'I'm keeping these things. I think you've wasted enough time on this emperor nonsense. You'd best go home and go back to digging ditches. Auctions have nothing to offer the likes of you.'

At first it looked as if Jan had no intention of obeying him, but Lars swung the cane once more and that was all it took to make the Emperor of Portugallia take to his heels and flee.

Not a soul moved to follow him, to offer a word of comfort or to call him back. In fact, most of the people couldn't stop themselves breaking into loud laughter when they saw the pitiful and dishonourable way he lost all his greatness.

This, however, was not to Lars Gunnarsson's taste. He liked his auctions to run with the same kind of solemnity as a church service.

'I believe it better to talk seriously to Jan than to laugh at him,' he said. 'Far too many people have played along with his madness and even called him emperor, but that's not the right way to deal with him. It would be much better to try to make him understand who he is, even if he doesn't particularly like it. I've been his employer for so long that it's my duty to see to it that he comes back to work. Otherwise he's going to end up as a burden on the parish.'

After that Lars ran a really fine auction at which the bids came thick and fast and the prices were high. Nor was the satisfaction he was feeling dimmed when he arrived home the following day and heard that Jan from Skrolycka had put on his working clothes and started ditching the fallow field.

'If we never mention his madness again,' Lars Gunnarsson said, 'perhaps he'll hang on to his sanity – he's got little enough anyway, so he needs what little he's got.'

The Catechetical Meeting

N othing had given Lars Gunnarsson more pleasure than taking away Jan's cane and leather cap and it rather looked as if by doing so he had also cured his madness.

A couple of weeks after the auction it was time for the annual catechetical meeting to be held at Falla Farm to allow the minister to check his parishioners' knowledge and understanding of the catechism. People from all round Lake Duvsjön attended, including the folk from Skrolycka. Unbelievable as it may seem, it was quite impossible to tell from looking at Jan that there had ever been any problems with his sanity!

Every bench and chair that Falla Farm possessed had been moved into the big room on the ground floor and the people arriving for the meeting filled the seats there. Jan was among them, but he made no effort to push forward to a better seat than the one allocated to him. Lars was keeping an eye on him the whole time and he had to concede that Jan's madness had indeed receded and he was behaving just like everyone else.

He was very quiet and anyone who greeted him received no more than a brief nod in response. That might, of course, have been because he didn't want to disrupt the solemnity of the meeting.

Before the catechising began, a register was taken of all those present, and when the minister called out the name of Jan Andersson from Skrolycka, Jan answered without any hesitation, as if Emperor Johannes of Portugallia had never existed.

The minister was sitting at a table at the top end of the room with the enormous register in front of him. Lars Gunnarsson was sitting beside him, assisting by informing him who had moved away from this catechetical district during the last year and who had got married.

Everyone noticed that after Jan had answered correctly and properly the minister turned to Lars and, speaking in a low voice, asked him a question.

'It wasn't as serious as it looked,' Lars answered. 'I drove it out of him, I did. And now he is back working here at Falla every day just as he has always done.'

Unlike the minister, Lars did not have the common sense to lower his voice. Everyone knew who he was talking about and many eyes turned on Jan, but he sat there calmly as if he had heard nothing.

When the questioning got under way the minister turned to one of the nervous young people whose knowledge of Christianity was being tested and asked them to recite the Fourth Commandment.

It was not completely accidental that the minister had chosen that particular commandment that evening. Here he was in the secure haven of a fine old farmhouse with benches along the walls and old-fashioned furnishings and clear signs of affluence wherever he looked. It was little wonder, then, that he felt inclined to remind his listeners of the benefits of sticking together generation after generation, allowing the older generation to be in charge for as long as they were capable, and then honouring and respecting them for the remainder of their years in this life.

He had just begun to elaborate on the great promises God made to those who honour their father and their mother when Jan from Skrolycka stood up.

'There's someone outside the door, afraid to come in,' he said.

'Börje,' the minister said, 'you are sitting closest to the door. Will you go and see what's going on?'

Börje stood up, opened the door and looked out into the hall.

'No, there's no one there,' he said. 'Jan must have been mistaken.'

The minister started the examination again. He explained to his listeners that this commandment was not so much an order as a piece of good advice that everyone should follow if they wanted life to go well. He himself was just a young man, the minister said, but he had already seen and experienced much that allowed him to state with certainty that disrespecting and disobeying one's parents lay behind many of the misfortunes in life.

While the minister was talking Jan turned his head towards the door time after time. He gestured to Kattrinna to go and open the door – she was sitting in the back row and it was easier for her to push her way through than for him. She stayed in her seat as long as possible, but being slightly afraid not to do what Jan wanted these days, she eventually obeyed him. When she opened the door, however, she could no more see anyone waiting in the hall than Börje had. She shook her head to Jan and went back to her seat.

The minister had not allowed Kattrinna to put him off his stride. To the great joy of the confirmands in his audience he had almost stopped asking questions and was devoting his efforts instead to telling them the beautiful thoughts that were thronging into his mind. 'Just think,' he said, 'how well and wisely we have arranged things for our dear old folk when we keep them with us in our homes! Is it not a sweet joy to support those who helped us when we were helpless, to make life easy for those who perhaps starved and froze so that we had bread? It is an honour for a young couple to have an aged father or mother sitting happy and comfortable ...'

As the minister said these words a quiet sobbing could be heard from a far corner of the room. Lars Gunnarsson, who had been sitting with his head bowed in piety, immediately stood up. He tiptoed across the floor so as not to disturb anyone, put his arm around his mother-in-law's waist and led her forward to the table at which the minister was sitting. She took over Lars Gunnarsson's chair while he stood behind and looked down at her. He also gestured to his wife and she came forward and stood on the other side of her mother. It looked beautiful. Everyone there understood that Lars was trying to show them that his home was just as the minister had said a home should be.

The minister looked relieved and pleased as he gazed at the old woman and her children. The only thing he found slightly unsettling was that the old woman was still weeping so copiously that she was at risk of floating away on her tears. In the past he had never succeeded in stirring such depths of emotion in one of his parishioners.

The minister continued. 'There is no difficulty, is there, in keeping the Fourth Commandment while we are young ourselves and obedient to our parents? But later, that's when it takes more effort. When we are adults and think that we are just as clever as ...'

At this point the minister was disturbed by Jan again. He had managed at last to push his way to the door and opened it.

Jan had more luck than the others and they heard him saying 'Good day' to someone out in the hall.

Everyone turned to look in the direction of the door to see who had been waiting outside, not daring to come in during the meeting. They heard Jan begging and coaxing and saw him open the door ajar, but whoever it was out there continued to raise objections. In the end, Jan just closed the door and came back in alone. But he didn't return to his seat. With great difficulty he pushed his way to the table where the minister was sitting.

'Well Jan,' the minister said rather impatiently, 'are you going to tell us who has been disturbing us the whole evening?'

'The old master here at Falla Farm was standing out there,' Jan announced without showing the least surprise or upset at what he was telling them. 'He didn't want to come in, but he asked me to pass a message to Lars that he should be on his guard on the first Sunday after midsummer.'

Only a few people understood at first what lay behind those words. The people on the benches at the back had been unable to hear properly, but they could see from the way the minister winced that Jan had said something terrible. They leapt to their feet and pressed forward, asking everyone and anyone who on earth Jan had brought a message from.

'But Jan!' the minister exclaimed in a stern voice. 'Do you know what you are saying?'

'I certainly do,' Jan said, nodding to the minister to confirm his words. 'I heard him out there all the time, didn't I? I asked him in but he wouldn't come. All he wanted was for a message to be passed to his son-in-law, and then he left. "Tell him," he said, "that it's not me who wishes him any harm for leaving me lying in my misery in the snow and not bringing help in time! But the Fourth Commandment is a stern commandment. Tell him from me that he had better repent and confess! He has the time between now and the Sunday after midsummer."'

Jan spoke so clearly and conveyed this remarkable message with such credibility that for some seconds the minister and the others present all believed that Farmer Erik of Falla Farm really had been outside the door of his old home and spoken to him. Inevitably all eyes turned to Lars Gunnarssson to see the effect Jan's words were having on him.

But Lars just stood there laughing. 'I believed Jan was sane,' he said, 'otherwise I wouldn't have let him attend this meeting. You must excuse the disturbance, minister. His madness is breaking out again.'

'Yes, it must be that!' the minister said, relieved. He wiped his brow: he'd come close to believing that he'd encountered something supernatural. It was good it had turned out to be no more than a madman's imagination.

'You see, minister, Jan doesn't have any great love for me,' Lars went on to explain. 'When his mind goes, he can't hold it back, and so it's coming out now. I have to admit that, rightly speaking, it's my fault his daughter had to go out into the world and earn money. That's what he can't forgive me for.'

The minister was surprised at Lars's urgent tone and gave him a searching look with his deep blue eyes. Lars looked away rather than meet his gaze. But then he realised that this looked bad and he made an effort to look the minister straight in the eye. He couldn't do it and he turned away with an oath.

'Lars Gunnarsson!' the minister exclaimed. 'What's got into you?'

Lars quickly pulled himself together. 'Is there no way I

can be rid of that fool?' he said, as if it was Jan he had sworn at. 'Here we are, and the minister and all my neighbours are thinking of me as a murderer just because a madman bears an old grudge against me. I tell you, it's because of his daughter that he wants to get at me. How was I to know that she would go off and fall by the wayside just because I wanted to be paid what I was owed? Isn't there anyone here who can take Jan in hand so that the rest of us can continue with our devotions?'

The minister ran his hand over his brow. Lars's words made him feel uncomfortable, but he couldn't risk admonishing him without being certain of the facts. He looked round for the old farmer's widow, but she had slipped away. Then he looked out over his congregation, but there was no guidance to be found there. He was certain that every single one of them knew whether Lars was guilty or not, but when the minister turned to them their faces seemed to close down and become expressionless. Kattrinna had come forward, taken Jan by the arm and they were on their way to the exit: the fool was the last person the minister wanted to question anyway.

'I think that will do for today,' he said quietly. 'Let's bring things to a close.'

He said a short prayer and they sang a hymn, after which all the visitors departed.

The minister was the last to leave. While escorting the minister to the gate, Lars broached what had just happened without being prompted. 'Did you notice, minister, that it was specifically on the Sunday after midsummer I should be on my guard? That proves it's the girl that Jan is thinking about. It was the Sunday after midsummer last year that I went to Jan's to arrange about the cottage.'

These explanations merely made the minister feel more and more uncomfortable. All of a sudden he placed his hand on Lars Gunnarsson's shoulder and tried to look him in the eye.

'Lars Gunnarsson!' he said in his most persuasive tone. 'I am not a judge. But you know that if you have something on your conscience you can come to me! I shall be expecting you, Lars Gunnarsson, every day. Just don't leave it too late.'

An Old Troll

Towards the end of the January of the second winter the little girl from Skrolycka was away from home, the weather became brutally cold. It was so severe that people were forced to shovel snow up over the small cottages in Askedalarna in an attempt to retain the heat. And people covered their cows with straw every night, frightened that they would freeze to death otherwise.

It was so cold that bread froze and cheese froze, so cold that even butter turned into a lump of ice. When the cold was at its worst even fire itself seemed incapable of staying hot. However much firewood was fed into the stove, the heat refused to spread beyond the edge of the fireplace.

One day when the cold was even more severe than before, Jan Andersson stayed at home to help Kattrinna keep the fire built up rather than going to work. Neither he nor his wife had risked going outdoors since morning, and the longer they stayed indoors the colder they felt. At about five o'clock when it began to grow dark, Kattrinna said they would be as well to go to bed. There was no point in staying up and suffering.

Jan had walked over to the window several times during the afternoon and looked out through the small corner of glass that was still clear. The rest of the panes were covered with thick ice flowers. He went over there once again and while standing there looking out he said to Kattrinna: 'You might as well go to bed, dear Kattrinna, but I'm going to stay up a while longer.'

'I will, then,' Kattrinna said. 'But why are you staying up? Why can't you come to bed with me?'

Jan did not answer the question directly. 'The strange thing is that I haven't seen Agrippa Prästberg walk past yet,' he said.

'Is that who you are waiting for?' Kattrinna said. 'Given the way he has behaved to you, you've no cause to stay up and freeze on his account.'

Jan gestured with his hand. Of all the mannerisms he had adopted during his time as emperor this was the only one he still occasionally used. There was no question of Prästberg visiting them, but Jan had heard that he'd been invited to a drinking session by one of the old Askedalarna fishermen and Jan was wondering why he hadn't seen him going past.

'He must have seen sense and stayed at home,' Kattrinna said.

As the day went on it became colder and colder. The joints and joists creaked as if the cold was knocking to be allowed entry. Bushes and trees were cloaked in such thick coats of snow and frost that their shape became indistinct; they, like everything else, had been forced to don whatever was available to protect them from the cold.

After a little while Kattrinna repeated her suggestion. 'I know it's only half-past five,' she said, 'but I'm going to put on the porridge pot and make supper. Then you can either go to bed or sit up and wait for Prästberg, as the mood takes you.'

Jan had not moved away from the window all this time. 'He can't have gone past without me seeing him,' he said.

'It can't really be of any importance to you whether a fellow like that comes or doesn't come,' Kattrinna said sharply, sick of hearing about the old vagrant.

Jan sighed a deep sigh. There was more truth in Kattrinna's words than she knew. Jan wasn't in the least interested whether old Grippa walked past or not. The only reason Jan had mentioned it was to have an excuse to stand by the window.

Since the day when Lars Gunnarsson had robbed him of his power and glory, Jan had received no sign or message from his little girl, the great empress. He knew that his loss could not have happened without her permission and consequently he understood that he must have done something to displease her. But for the life of him, he could not work out what it was.

He pondered on it through the long winter nights, through the long dark mornings when he was threshing in the barn at Falla, during the short hours of daylight when he was bringing down logs from the forest.

He couldn't believe she had disliked the idea of him being emperor. After all, everything had gone so well and so happily for three whole months. It had been a time such as a poor man like Jan could never have dreamt of experiencing. Klara surely couldn't have had any objection to that.

So he must have done or said something that displeased her and that was why he was being punished.

But she surely couldn't be so merciless as never to forgive him, could she? If only she would tell him why she was angry and what he had to do to be reconciled with her, he would do it – and do it without complaint. She must know that he had put on his working clothes and gone back to labouring the moment she had let him know that was what she wanted.

He did not want to talk about the situation with Kattrinna or with the net maker. He would be patient and wait until he received a sure sign from Klara. There were many times when he felt it was so close that he only had to stretch out his hand and he would touch it.

And this very day when he had been trapped indoors he had felt certain that news from Klara was approaching. That was why he was standing peering out through the small clear corner of the window pane. He had a feeling that if he did not receive news soon, life would quickly become more than he could bear.

By this time it was so dark that he could scarcely see as far as the gate, so hope was over for the day. He made no further objection to the suggestion they go to bed. Kattrinna made porridge, they ate supper and by quarter past six they were in bed.

They went to sleep quickly, but they did not sleep long. The big Mora clock had only just reached half past six when Jan leapt out of bed. He quickly put firewood on the fire, which had not yet gone out, and started to dress.

He tried to be as quiet as possible but he couldn't avoid

waking Kattrinna. She sat up and asked whether it was already morning.

No, it certainly wasn't. But his little girl had called him in a dream and ordered him to go up to the forest.

Now it was Kattrinna's turn to sigh. His madness must be coming back. Jan had been so depressed and uneasy of late that she had been expecting this every day.

She made no effort to convince him to stay at home and, instead, she rose and began dressing too.

'Wait a moment!' she said when Jan was already at the door and about to go out. 'If you are going up into the forest tonight, I am coming with you.'

She had been expecting Jan to offer some objection, but he did not. He waited at the door until she was ready. He seemed to be in a great hurry, although he was being more reasonable and sensible now than earlier in the day.

It was no evening to be out of doors! The cold hit them like a wall of sharp, searing splinters of glass. It pierced their skin and they felt as if their noses were being torn from their faces; the tips of their fingers ached and they couldn't feel whether they still had toes.

But neither Jan nor Kattrinna made a sound of complaint, they just pushed on. Jan turned off onto the winter road over the hill, the same one he had taken with Klara one Christmas morning when she was so small he had to carry her.

The sky was clear and a slim, white sliver of moon gleamed in the west, so it was far from dark. Keeping to the road was nevertheless difficult because everything was so white, and time after time they strayed out to the edge and sank deep into snowdrifts.

They managed somehow to struggle on as far as the great boulder that a giant of old had hurled at Svartsjö church. Jan was already past it when Kattrinna, who was behind him, suddenly cried out.

'Jan!' she shouted. Jan hadn't heard her sound so frightened since the day Lars had come to take their cottage from them. 'Look! Don't you see? There's someone sitting there!'

Jan turned and went back to her, and then the two of them,

both Jan and Kattrinna, very nearly took to their heels. There, before their very eyes, its back against the boulder and almost completely coated with white rime frost, sat a big old troll with a bushy beard and a long, trunk-like nose.

It was sitting there utterly motionless and the only explanation could be that the cold had frozen it so stiff that it hadn't been able to make it back to its underground lair or wherever it was that it lived.

'Who'd have thought such creatures still existed!' Kattrinna said. 'I'd have never believed it, even though I've heard a lot of talk about them.'

Jan rather than Kattrinna was the first of them to calm down and recognise what they were actually looking at.

'It's not a troll, Kattrinna,' he said. 'That's Agrippa Prästberg.'

'Dear Lord, what are you saying?' Kattrinna exclaimed. 'The way he looks, it's easy to make a mistake!'

'He must have sat down and gone to sleep. Let's hope he's not dead!'

They shouted the old man's name and they shook him, but he remained rigid and motionless.

'Run back for the sledge so that we can drag him home!' Jan said. 'I'll stay here and rub him with snow until he wakes up.'

'As long as you don't freeze to death too,' Kattrinna said.

'My dear Kattrinna,' Jan said, 'I haven't been as warm as I am tonight for many a day. I'm so happy about our little girl. Wasn't it wonderful of her to send us out to save the life of the man who's been going around spreading so many lies about her?'

*

A couple of weeks later, just as Jan was setting off home from work, Agrippa Prästberg came up to him.

'I'm hale and hearty again now,' Grippa said, 'but I realise that if you and Kattrinna hadn't come to help me there wouldn't be much left of Johan Utter Agrippa Prästberg. I've been wondering what I could do for you in return.'

'Don't even think about it, Agrippa Prästberg, my good fellow,' Jan said, waving the suggestion away.

'Be quiet and listen to me!' Prästberg said. 'When I say I'm thinking of doing something in return, it's not just empty chatter with nothing to back it up. I've seen to it already. The other day I met the pedlar who gave your lass the red dress.'

'Who?' Jan said, becoming so excited that he started to gasp for breath.

'The fellow who gave the lass the dress and then got her into trouble in Stockholm. The first thing I did was to give him such a beating on your behalf that he couldn't take any more. Then I told him he'd get more of the same the next time he showed his face around here.'

Jan couldn't believe that he was hearing properly.

'But what did he say? Didn't you ask him about Klara? Didn't he bring any word from her?'

'What was he supposed to say? He took his beating and he said nothing. Now I've repaid you and we are quits. Johan Utter Agrippa Prästberg doesn't believe in having debts.'

He marched off, leaving Jan standing in the road moaning loudly. His little girl, his little girl! She had been trying to send word to him and this pedlar must have been carrying a message from her. But now the man had been driven away and Jan would learn nothing.

Jan did not weep. He wrung his hands, and every part of his body ached worse than if he had been ill.

He realised that Klara's intention had been for Prästberg, who was always out and about on the roads, to receive a message from the pedlar and pass it on to Jan. But there was clearly no difference between Prästberg and a troll: whether they tried to be a help or a hindrance, misfortune was the inevitable result.

The Sunday after Midsummer

On the first Sunday after midsummer all the people in Askedalarna were invited to the net maker's place for a big party that Ol Bengtsa and his daughter-in-law always held at that time of year.

We might well wonder why two such poverty-stricken people would hold a party every year, but those who knew the reason found it a natural enough thing to do.

This is how it had come about. Back in the days when the net maker had been a rich man he had given each of his two sons a farm. The older of the two had managed his property in more or less the same way as Ol Bengtsa had done and consequently died a pauper. The other son was steadier and more organised. He not only held on to his gift, he actually increased it and became quite prosperous.

What he owned, however, was next to nothing compared to what he would have had if his father hadn't behaved with such foolhardy extravagance and disposed of both money and property as if there was no future to worry about. If wealth of that sort had come into the son's hands in his early youth, there is no telling how far he would have gone. He might have owned all the forests in the Lövsjö district, the shop in Broby and the steamer on Lake Löven. He might even have been ironmaster at the Ekeby ironworks.

Naturally enough, this son found his father's mis-management difficult to forgive, but he always kept his feelings in check and there had been no breach between them. When Ol Bengtsa's affairs went to pieces, a great many people – including Ol Bengtsa himself – had expected the son to use his resources to help him, but what would have been the point? Everything would just have gone to the creditors anyway. And it was, in fact, with the idea that his father would have something to fall back on that the son hung on to what he had been given.

It wasn't the younger son's fault that Ol Bengtsa had then gone to live with his elder son's widow and offered to support her by making nets. The younger son had asked his father to come and live with him, and if he asked once he had asked a hundred times. This, in a sense, was the cause of another injustice in that the son's reputation suffered among people who knew what a hard time the old man was having.

But even that had failed to sow dissension between father and son and, as a demonstration of his friendship, once every summer the son and his wife and children travelled the dangerous road over to Askedalarna and stayed there a whole day.

If people had only known how troubled both he and his wife felt every time they saw the little cottage and the miserable hovel of an outhouse and the stony potato patch and their sister-in-law's ragged children, they would have understood the depth of affection for his father he revealed by putting himself through this annual visit.

The worst thing of all, so both he and his wife thought, was that a party was laid on for them. Every year as they left for home they begged and pleaded with him not to invite all the neighbours to a celebration the following year, but the old man was not to be moved. He did not want to desist from holding a party even though he most certainly could not afford it. You wouldn't have believed there was much left of the old Ol Bengtsa of Ljusterbyn when you saw how old and worn out he now looked, but he still retained the urge to spend in a big way. That is what had caused his misfortune and he seemed unable to free himself from it.

His son had heard indirectly, and he could see it for himself anyway, that the old man and his sister-in-law scraped and saved for the whole year to lay on a worthy celebration on the day of his visit. There was food and yet more food. Coffee and a generous helping of sandwiches before they were even out of the carriage. Then dinner for all the neighbours: fish and meat and rice pudding cake and fruit syrup pudding and copious quantities of drink. It was enough to make you weep. The son and his wife did nothing to encourage this madness. The only food and drink they brought along was ordinary, everyday food, but they still couldn't avoid the party.

There were times when they said to each other that the only way of preventing their father ruining himself for a second time was for them to stop visiting. But they were afraid that no one would understand that their reasons for staying at home were the very best ones.

And then there was the company they had to keep at these parties. Aged blacksmiths and fishermen and cottars. If it hadn't been for the fact that the respectable enough people from Falla Farm usually came, there wouldn't have been a soul for them to talk to.

Ol Bengtsa's son had been particularly fond of Farmer Erik, but he also had quite a high opinion of Lars Gunnarsson, who had taken over the farm after his father-in-law's death. Lars wasn't from a prominent family, but he was a man who'd had the sense to make a good marriage and would probably elbow his way to wealth and reputation before the game was over.

It was thus a great disappointment to arrive in Askedalarna in the third year after Farmer Erik's death and be told the moment he arrived that Lars Gunnarsson probably wouldn't be coming to the party this time.

'It's not my fault,' the old net maker said. 'He is not exactly one of my people, but I went over to Falla Farm yesterday to invite him specially for you.'

'Maybe he's tired of these parties,' his son said.

'No, it's not that,' the old man said. 'I do believe he would have liked to be here, but something else was stopping him.'

The old net maker did not offer any further explanation of what he meant, but they hadn't even finished their first cups of coffee before he returned to the topic.

'Don't be too sad that Lars isn't coming this evening,' he said. 'There's no guarantee you would enjoy his company nowadays, as he has been rather out of order recently.'

'You don't mean that he's taken to drink, do you?' his son said.

'That's not a bad guess,' the old man said. 'It started during the spring and I don't think he's been sober a single day since midsummer.'

What usually happened on these visits was that, once they had drunk their coffee, father and son would take their rods and go to the lake to fish. While fishing the old man usually kept absolutely quiet so as not to frighten the fish, but this year was different.

Time after time he started conversations with his son. As usual it was all a bit slow, of course, and the sentences were brief, but it was obvious that there was more life in the old man than in previous years.

It was as if there was something special he wanted to bring into the open or, to be more accurate, that there was something he wanted his son to give him an answer to. He was like a man standing outside an empty house shouting and calling and reluctant to give up hope that someone will come and open the door.

He returned to the subject of Lars Gunnarsson several times. He told his son about the recent catechetical meeting and he also mentioned the gossip about Lars that had circulated round Askedalarna after the death of Farmer Erik.

His son agreed that Lars might well not have been completely innocent. The fact he had started drinking was certainly a bad sign.

'I am really curious as to how he is going to get through this day,' the old net maker said.

Just at that moment his son got a bite, so he didn't need to give an answer. Now, of course, there was nothing in this story that resembled the relationship between him and his father, but he couldn't help thinking that the old man was trying to give a particular meaning to what he was saying.

'I hope he goes to the minister this evening,' the old man said. 'There is forgiveness, but only for those who seek it.'

This was followed by a long silence. His son was busy re-baiting his hook with a new worm and didn't answer. And, when all was said and done, there was nothing there that needed an answer. But then the old man sighed so deeply that his son had to turn and look at him.

'Haven't you noticed that you've got a bite, Father?' he said. 'You are not going to let that perch pull the rod from your hands, are you?'

The old man jumped and began taking the fish off the hook, but he fumbled so much that the fish fell back into the lake.

'I shan't be catching any fish today however much I want to,' he said.

Yes, there was definitely something he wanted to hear from his son's lips. But he could hardly be expecting him to compare himself to someone suspected of having killed his father-in-law, could he?

The old man did not put a new worm on his hook. He was standing on a rock with his hands together, his dull eyes staring out over the shining water.

'Yes, there is forgiveness,' he said. 'For those who leave the old to freeze to death in the icy cold, there is forgiveness unto this very day. But then it's over.'

This could hardly have been directed at his son, could it? The old man must have been thinking aloud, as old people often do.

Anyway, it occurred to his son to try to move the conversation on to something else.

'How are things with that local fellow who went mad last autumn?' he asked.

'You mean Jan at Skrolycka?' the old man said. 'He's been in his right mind the whole winter. He doesn't intend to come to the party today either, but he's a poor cotter, just like me, so I don't suppose you'll miss him.'

That may well have been true, but his son was so glad to talk about anyone other than Lars Gunnarsson that, with great show of sympathy, he asked what had been the matter with Jan at Skrolycka.

'Him? He missed his daughter so much it made him ill, that's all. She left home two years ago and they haven't heard a word from her since!'

'The girl who has fallen into misfortune?'

'Aha, you remember it then. But that's not the reason her father is grieving to death. What he can't bear is the great lovelessness.'

This desire to talk was too worrying. His father was talking more than was good for him.

'Do you know what? I think I'll go out on that far rock,' his son said. 'I can see the fish rising around it.'

This move took him out of earshot and there was no more conversation between them for the rest of the morning. But wherever the son went, he could feel those dim, dull eyes following him.

For once he was glad when the guests arrived.

A table was laid outside the cottage and when the old net maker sat down at the dinner table he did his best to put aside all his sorrows and cares. When he sat there as host, enough of the old Ol Bengtsa emerged for people to see more or less what kind of man he had been in the past.

No one from Falla Farm was present, but it was quite obvious that Lars Gunnarsson was on everyone's mind. That, of course, was hardly to be wondered at since this was the very day Lars had been warned about. Ol Bengtsa's son had to listen to one account after another about that evening meeting at Falla Farm and how strange it was that the minister had chosen that particular evening to talk about one's duty to parents. Ol Bengtsa must have seen from his son's expression that he was bored by it all, even though he was saying nothing. So he turned to him and said:

'What do you have to say about all this, Nils? I've no doubt you are sitting there thinking to yourself how strange it is that Our Lord failed to write a commandment telling parents how to behave towards their children.'

This took his son by surprise. He felt his face flushing as if he had been caught red-handed.

'But my dear Father,' he said. 'I have neither thought nor said ...'

'No, you haven't. That's true,' his father interrupted him. He then turned to the people sitting at the table and said: 'I know it will be difficult for you to believe, but the truth is that neither my son nor his wife has ever said a harsh word to me.'

The old man hadn't directed these words to anyone in particular and none of those present felt like taking it upon themselves to answer him.

'They had to undergo a hard test, though,' Ol Bengtsa continued. 'They lost the chance of large properties. They could have been gentry by now if I had behaved properly. But they have never said a thing. And they come to visit me every summer to show that they aren't angry with me.'

The old man's face was dead now, quite dead, and his voice quiet. His son did not know whether he was working his way to saying something in particular or whether he was just talking in order to have something to say.

'It's a different matter with Lisa here,' the old man said, pointing to the daughter-in-law he lived with. 'She moans at me every day for having destroyed my fortune.'

The daughter-in-law was not in the least put out and she responded with a good-humoured laugh: 'And you moan at me for not getting round to patching all the holes in the boys' clothes.'

'That's true,' the old man conceded. 'The point is that we're not shy with one another, we speak out. We can talk about everything, and everything that is mine is hers and everything that is hers is mine. So I'm starting to believe that she's the one who's my real child.'

His son became embarrassed again, and anxious too. The old net maker was trying to force something out into the open. He was waiting for an answer of some kind. But he surely couldn't be asking for it to come out here among all these guests.

It came as an enormous relief to Ol Bengtsa's son when he looked up and saw Lars Gunnarsson and his wife standing at the gate about to come into the yard. And he wasn't the only one to feel like that; everyone present was pleased Lars and his wife had come. It seemed they had all forgotten their dark suspicions.

Lars and his wife apologised repeatedly for arriving late.

Lars had been suffering from a bad headache and they had thought they wouldn't be able to come at all. But the headache had eased a little and so he thought he'd try to join the festivities. Perhaps he would forget the pain if he went out and about among people.

Lars had lost some hair and there were dark rings around his eyes, but he was as cheerful and sociable as he'd been the year before. He'd barely had time to eat a mouthful before he and Ol Bengtsa's son were talking forestry business, discussing big profits and money they had out on loan.

The ordinary little people around them were astonished at the large sums mentioned and were afraid to say anything. Ol Bengtsa was the only one prepared to say a word.

'Since you're talking about money, Nils,' he said, 'I wonder if you remember the promissory note for 17,000 riksdaler I had from the old ironmaster at Duvnäs. You'll remember that it was mislaid and I couldn't find it when I needed it most. I wrote to the ironmaster and asked for my money anyway, but received the answer that he was on his deathbed. And when he was dead, his executors could find nothing about the debt in his books, so they informed me it was impossible to pay since I couldn't produce the promissory note. We hunted for it, both me and my sons, but we never did find it.'

'You're not going to tell me that you've found it now, are you?' his son exclaimed.

'It's amazing – more than amazing,' the old man continued. 'Jan from Skrolycka came here one morning and told me that he definitely knew that the note was in a secret drawer in my clothes chest. He had dreamt he saw me taking it out.'

'But you'd already searched there, hadn't you?'

'I had. I'd looked in the secret drawer on the left side of the chest, but Jan told me it would be on the right. And when I looked I found a secret drawer on that side that I'd never known about. And that's where the note was.'

'You must presumably have put it in that side at some point when you were drunk and confused,' his son said.

'Yes, that's what I must have done, I suppose,' the old man conceded.

His son put down his knife and fork for a moment, but then he picked them up again. There was something in the old man's voice that sounded a warning note. Perhaps this was all a lie?

'It was presumably out-of-date?' he said.

'Yes – or it certainly would have been with any other debtor. I rowed down and showed it to the young master at Duvnäs and he immediately admitted it was right. "It's as clear as the light of day that I must pay my father's debt to you, Ol Bengtsa," he said. "But you'll have to give me a couple of weeks' grace. It's a big sum to pay out all at once."'

'Spoken like a man of honour,' his son said, placing his hand heavily on the table. Despite his suspicions, joy was beginning to seep surreptitiously through his veins. So this was it! This was the great news his father had been holding back all day and had felt unable to broach!

'I told the master he didn't need to pay anything,' the net maker said. 'As long as he gave me another promissory note, he could hang on to the money as far as I was concerned.'

'That wasn't such a bad idea,' his son said. He was finding it difficult to look as calm as seemed desirable in the circumstances. He knew that it was impossible to be sure of anything when dealing with Ol Bengtsa – the next moment he might take it into his head to say that he had made it all up.

'You don't believe me, do you?' the old man said. 'Do you want to see the note? Lisa, go in and fetch it, will you?'

In no time at all the old man's son was studying the promissory note. He looked first at the signature and he recognised the clear, legible writing immediately. Then he looked at the figures and they were also correct. He nodded to his wife, who was sitting opposite him, that everything was as it should be, and then he passed the note across to her because he realised how impatient she would be to look at it.

His wife read the note carefully from start to finish.

'What's this?' she said. '"Pay Lisa Persdotter of Askedalarna, widow of Bengt Olsson from Ljusterbyn" – is the promissory note made out to Lisa?'

'Yes,' the old man said. 'She is to have that money from me

because she is my true child.'

'But it's unjust to ...'

'No,' the old man said in his weary voice, 'it is not unjust. I have done the right thing and I don't owe anyone anything.' And turning to his son he continued: 'There might have been someone else I owed something to, but I've checked that and I know now there is no one else.'

'You mean me, don't you?' his son said. 'You never think of me ...'

Whatever it was that the son was about to say to his father remained unsaid. He was interrupted by a loud cry from the other side of the table.

Lars Gunnarsson had suddenly grabbed a full bottle of snaps and put it to his lips. His wife shrieked in horror and tried to take the bottle from him.

He held her at arm's length until he had emptied half the bottle. Then he put the bottle back on the table and turned to his wife. Red in the face and wild-eyed he stood wringing his hands.

'Did you hear that?' he said. 'It was Jan who found the note. Everything he dreams is true. He can see the future. You wait and see – misfortune will strike me today, just as he said.'

'But all he said to you was that you should be on your guard!'

'You begged me to come here today in order to forget what day it is. And instead of that I've been given a reminder!'

He raised the bottle to his lips again while his wife threw herself at him with tears and entreaties. He put it down on the table with a laugh.

'Keep it! You're welcome to it as far as I'm concerned!' he said, standing up and kicking a chair away. 'Goodbye Ol Bengtsa! You'll excuse me, I hope, if I go? Today I need to be somewhere I can drink in peace.'

He walked towards the gate, his wife following him.

As he went through the open gate he pushed her back.

'What do you want with me? I've had my warning. I'm going to my doom.'

Summer Night

J an at Skrolycka stayed indoors the whole day of the big
party over at the net maker's place, but when evening
came he went outside and sat in his usual place on the
stone slab by the door. He wasn't ill so much as feeling
weak and low, and the cottage was so hot after the long sunny
day that he thought it would be good to get some fresh air.
It quickly became apparent that there wasn't much cool to be
had outside either, but he stayed out there anyway, mainly
because there were so many magnificent things to look at.

June had been an unbelievably hot and dry month and the
forest fires that broke out every dry summer were already
raging. He could tell what was happening from the banks of
beautiful, blue-white smoke rising above the Duvsjö Hills on
the other side of the lake. And soon he could also see gleaming
white curls of cloud far to the south, and when he looked west
towards Storsnipa there were clouds mixed with smoke rising
high above the hill there too. The whole world seemed to be
on fire.

From where he was sitting he couldn't see flames, but even
without that it was frightening to know that fire had broken
out and could rage at will. He could only hope it would be
satisfied with the trees of the forest and not find its way to
attack cottages and farms.

Breathing was difficult. So much air seemed to have been
consumed by the fire that there was little left. Every so often
the smell of burning caught in his throat. It wasn't coming
from any of the stoves in Askedalarna, it was a greeting from
the great blaze of moss and brushwood and pine needles that
was roaring and spitting a dozen miles away.

A little while earlier the sun had set, fiery red. It had left enough colour to paint the whole sky pale crimson, not just where the sun had gone down, but across the whole horizon. At the same time, the waters of Lake Duvsjön below the steep Duvsjö Hills became as black as mirror glass, and the blackness was shot with streaks of red blood and gleaming gold.

It was the kind of night when we feel that the earth does not deserve as much as a glance. It is only the sky and the waters that mirror the sky that are worthy of being looked at.

As Jan sat there gazing at all this magnificence, something happened to make him wonder. It seemed unlikely that he was seeing it properly, but he had the impression that the vault of the heavens was beginning to sink lower. To his eyes at least, it had come much closer to earth than usual.

It's impossible for something to have gone wrong, he thought. Nor could his eyes be faulty. It really was true – the great, pale red vault was moving down closer to the earth. The suffocating warmth grew and he was on the point of passing out. He could already feel the immense heat emanating from the furnace of the dome that was sinking down towards him.

Jan had, of course, often heard that there would come a time when the earth would perish, and he had often thought it would be marked by powerful thunderstorms and earthquakes that would hurl the mountains into the lakes, forcing the waters of the lakes up over the valleys and plains so that everything living would perish. But he had never thought the end would come like this, with the earth buried beneath the vault of the heavens and people smothered and dying of heat. This, he thought, must be worse than anything else.

He put down his pipe though it was only half-smoked, but apart from that he did not move from the spot. What else could he do? This was not an event it was possible to avert, nor was it possible to escape. There were no weapons with which you could defend yourself, nor was there a hiding place to creep into. If all the seas and lakes were emptied, their waters would not be enough to slake the heat of the heavenly vault. If all the mountains were torn up by their roots and used as pillars, they would not be capable of holding up that heavy vault if it was meant to sink.

What was so strange, however, was that he and he alone had noticed what was going on.

But look! What was that rising above the mountain ridges? A host of black spots visible against the light clouds of smoke? Moving so fast that they made short black streaks before his eyes, rather like a swarm of bees.

Birds, of course! But the remarkable thing was that they had risen from their nocturnal roosts and flown into the air in the middle of the night.

They knew much more than people knew. They had sensed that something was happening.

The air did not cool as it would have done on any other night, instead it grew hotter and hotter. But that was only to be expected, for the red vault was approaching ever closer. Jan thought it had already sunk so low that it was touching the brow of Storsnipa far above him.

If the end of the world was so close, if there was no longer any hope of a message from Klara, far less any chance of seeing her before the end, he would pray for just one mercy: to be allowed to understand what he had done to cross her, so that he could make up for it before all things of this earth came to an end. What had he done that she could not forget and forgive? Why had the imperial treasures been taken from him?

As he asked these questions his eyes fell on a small piece of gold paper glittering on the ground in front of him. It gleamed and shone as if trying to catch his attention, though his mind was no longer on such things. It must have come from one of the stars he had borrowed from Daft-Ingborg, but he had put such vanity behind him throughout the winter.

It was becoming ever hotter and ever more difficult to breathe. The end was coming and it was probably good that it would be very soon now.

He felt a great weakness seeping through his body and, no longer able to sit upright, he slipped down from the stone and stretched out on the ground.

It wasn't fair to Kattrinna that he didn't tell her what was happening, but she wasn't at home, she was still at the net maker's party. If he'd had the energy to drag himself there, he would have liked to say a word of farewell to Ol Bengtsa too.

So he was glad, truly glad, to see Kattrinna approaching, accompanied by the net maker. He wanted to call out to them to hurry, but he was no longer capable of uttering a word. And then the two of them were bending over him.

Kattrinna went to fetch water for him, and that gave him enough strength to tell them that the last judgment was upon them.

'Go on with you!' Kattrinna said. 'The last judgment! It's you, you have a fever and you're delirious.'

Jan turned to the net maker. 'Can't you see it either, Ol Bengtsa? Can't you see the vault of the heavens sinking?'

The net maker did not answer and, turning to Kattrinna, he said:

'This is not going to turn out well. I think we'll have to try to do what we were talking about on the way here. It would be best if I go to Falla at once.'

'I'm sure Lars will raise objections, though,' Kattrinna said.

'But Lars has gone to the inn. And I think Farmer Erik's widow will pluck up courage and ...'

Jan interrupted him. He couldn't bear hearing them talk of worldly things when such great events were approaching. 'Say no more!' he said. 'Do you not hear the last trump? Do you not hear it thundering in the mountains?'

They paused and listened for a moment as Jan had asked them to do, and now they noticed that they, too, could hear something unusual.

'There's a cart of some sort crashing through the forest,' Kattrinna said. 'What on earth can that be?'

They became more and more baffled as the sound came closer.

'It's Sunday evening,' Kattrinna said. 'If it was an ordinary working day, I could understand, but who would be driving a cart along the forest road on a Sunday night?'

She stopped talking again in order to listen and they could

hear the wheels scraping over rocks and the horse's hooves skidding as they descended the steep slopes.

'Do you hear?' Jan said. 'Do you hear?'

'Yes, I can hear,' Kattrinna said. 'But it's no concern of mine what it is. My first job is to get you into bed, that's what I have to think about.'

'Yes, and I must go to Falla Farm,' the net maker said. 'That's the most important thing of all. Goodbye! I'll be back!'

The old net maker hurried off as fast as he could go and Kattrinna went into the cottage to make up a bed. No sooner had she gone in than the clatter which she and the net maker thought was coming from an ordinary cart was almost upon them. As it approached the whole earth trembled with the thundering of heavy chariots. Jan called loudly for Kattrinna and she came rushing out.

'Dear Jan, don't be afraid,' she said. 'I can see the horse now. It's only old Bruning from Falla Farm. Sit up so you can see too.'

She put her arm behind Jan's head and raised it for him to see. Through the alder shrubs that lined the road Jan caught a glimpse of a horse galloping wildly towards Skrolycka.

'Do you see now?' Kattrinna said. 'It's only Lars Gunnarsson driving home. He's been at the inn and he's so drunk he doesn't know which road he's taken.'

As she said this, the cart rattled past their gate and they had a better view of it. Both Jan and Kattrinna could see that the cart was empty and there was no one at the reins.

All at once Kattrinna gave a scream and pulled her arm away so quickly that Jan fell back with a thud.

'God deliver us!' she said. 'Did you see him, Jan? He was being dragged along!'

She didn't wait for an answer. She ran across the yard and down the road along which the horse had bolted.

Jan made no objection to her going. He was glad to be alone again. He still had no answer to why the empress was angry with him.

The small piece of gold paper now lay in his direct line of sight and it was gleaming so much that he had to look at it once more. The piece of paper led his thoughts to Daft-Ingborg and the time he had met her at Borg Landing.

And now it struck him that here was the answer to his question. Now he knew what it was that had displeased his little girl throughout the winter. He had been unjust to Daft-Ingborg! He should never have refused her wish to accompany the empress to Portugallia.

How could he have had such a poor opinion of the great empress as to assume she would not want Daft-Ingborg with her! It was precisely people like Ingborg she most wanted to help.

No wonder she had been angry. He really ought to have understood that the poor and the unhappy would always be welcome in her realm.

There wasn't much he could do about it if there was to be no tomorrow. But what if there was a tomorrow! If so, the first thing he would do was go and talk to Daft-Ingborg.

He closed his eyes and folded his hands. To put this anxiety to rest was sweet: dying was so much easier now.

He didn't know how much time passed before he heard Kattrinna's voice close beside him.

'Dear Jan, how are you? You're not going to die and leave me, are you?'

She sounded so anxious that he had to make the effort to open his eyes.

And he saw that Kattrinna was holding the imperial cane and his green leather cap.

'I asked the people at Falla Farm to let me bring them to you. I told them that, whatever happens, it would be better for you to have them than that you lose the will to live.'

Jan put his hands together.

His little girl, the great empress, was truly remarkable. No sooner had he recognised his sin and promised to atone for it than she took him into her grace and favour once more.

He felt an enormous sense of relief. The vault of the heavens was rising and, as it rose, it was taking the great heat with it and allowing air to enter. He felt strong enough to rise to his feet and reach for his imperial treasures.

'You can have them in peace now,' Kattrinna said. 'No one will come and take them away from you again, for Lars Gunnarsson is dead.'

The Emperor's Wife

Kattrinna from Skrolycka had come to the kitchen at Lövdala Manor with spun yarn. Mrs Liljekrona herself took the yarn, weighed it, paid Kattrinna and praised her work.

'It's just as well you are a good worker, Kattrinna,' she said. 'You have to earn the daily bread for yourself and your husband these days.'

Kattrinna drew herself up a little and a touch of colour rushed to her face, just above her prominent cheekbones.

'Jan tries,' she said, 'but he has never had the strength of an ordinary working man.'

'But he is not doing anything at all, is he?' Mrs Liljekrona said. 'I have heard he spends his time running around from one farm to the next showing off his stars and singing songs.'

Mrs Liljekrona was a serious and conscientious woman and she liked other hard-working and industrious people like Kattrinna from Skrolycka. She felt sympathy for her and was trying to show it.

But Kattrinna continued to defend her husband.

'He is old, and he has had a great deal of sorrow in recent years. He deserves some freedom after a lifetime of hard labour.'

'It's a good thing you can take your misfortune so calmly, Kattrinna,' Mrs Liljekrona said, a touch of sharpness in her voice. 'But I really do think that you, being such a sensible person, should try to get Jan to give up these delusions of his. Believe me, if it's allowed to go on like this we shall end up having to commit him to the asylum.'

Kattrinna stood up and looked offended.

'Jan is not mad,' she said. 'Our Lord has put blinkers on him so he doesn't have to see the things he can't bear to see. We can be thankful for that.'

Mrs Liljekrona had no desire to be dogmatic. And she also thought it was only right and proper that a wife took her husband's side. 'Well, in that case everything is fine as it is, Kattrinna,' she said in a kindly voice. 'And don't forget that there's always work for you here all year round.'

All at once the stern old face in front of her softened and crumpled. Everything holding Kattrinna together gave way, and sorrow and anxiety and love came to the surface, and her eyes overflowed.

'My only joy is struggling for him,' she said. 'He has become so strange over the years – as if he is more than just a human being. And that will probably be the reason they take him away from me.'

IV.

The Welcome

She had come, his little girl had come. It is hard to find words to describe the great event.

She came so late in the autumn that the passenger steamers on Lake Löven were no longer running and the only traffic on the lake was a couple of small cargo boats. She had not wanted to travel that way, or perhaps she didn't even know they existed, and so she had taken a carriage to Askedalarna from the railway station, which meant that Jan could not meet her at Borg Landing where he had waited for the past fifteen years. She had been his when she was still at home, bringing him joy for eighteen years; and for almost as long again he had had to be without her.

He didn't even have the good fortune to be at home in their cottage to greet her when she arrived. He had just gone off to spend time talking to the old Falla widow, who had moved out of the main house and lived on her own. She was one of the many lonely old people the Emperor of Portugallia had to visit now and again to have a friendly chat and to keep up their spirits.

It was only Kattrinna who was standing at the door to receive her when the little girl returned home. Kattrinna had been sitting at the spinning wheel all day and she had just stopped the wheel to take a short rest when she heard the sound of a carriage coming along the road. For anyone to drive through Askedalarna was a sufficiently unusual event for Kattrinna to go to the door and listen, and she could hear it wasn't just an ordinary working cart, it was a gig. Kattrinna's hands immediately began to tremble. They had a tendency to do that these days whenever something frightened or upset her, but otherwise she was hale and hearty and a good worker in spite of her seventy-two years. But she did worry that the trembling hands might get worse and make it impossible for her to earn a living for Jan and herself as she'd been able to do until then.

Over the years Kattrinna had given up hope of ever seeing her daughter again and she hadn't thought about her at all that day. But she said later that from the moment she heard the gig she knew for certain who was coming. She went to the chest of drawers to fetch a clean apron, but her hands were shaking so much that she couldn't put the key in the keyhole. She was unable to tidy herself up and had to go out and welcome her daughter in what she had on.

The little girl did not arrive in a golden vessel, she wasn't even sitting up on the gig, she was walking. The road to Askedalarna was as bad now as it had been when Farmer Erik and his wife had driven her to the minister's to be baptised, and now she and the driver were walking one on each side of the gig, holding on to the two large trunks loaded behind the seat to stop them being shaken off into the ditch. Her arrival was no grander than that, and more was perhaps not to be expected.

Kattrinna had just opened the front door when the gig stopped at the gate. She should, of course, have run to open it, but she didn't. She suddenly felt such a weight pressing on her chest that she was unable to take a step.

It was Klara, she knew it was, even though the woman opening the gate looked like a gentlewoman. She was wearing a hat with feathers and flowers and her clothes were of fine materials, but it was the little girl from Skrolycka, there was no doubting that.

She hurried into the yard ahead of the gig and approached Kattrinna with her hand outstretched. But Kattrinna remained motionless, her eyes closed. So much bitterness was rising within her at that moment. She felt she couldn't forgive her daughter for being alive and for coming home so healthy and well after letting them wait in vain for all those years. She almost wished her daughter had not bothered to come.

She must have looked close to collapse for Klara quickly threw her arms around her and almost carried her into the cottage. 'Dear, dear Mother, you mustn't be so fearful,' she said. 'Don't you recognise me?'

Kattrinna opened her eyes and studied her closely. She was a sensible woman and she had not expected someone who has been away for fifteen years to look the same as when she left home, but she was horrified by what she saw.

The woman facing her looked much older than she should have looked. Klara was, after all, only a little over thirty years old. But it wasn't the hair that was grey at the temples and the lined forehead that shocked Kattrinna, it was because Klara had grown ugly. There was a peculiar greyish-yellow tinge to her complexion and something thick and coarse about her mouth. The whites of her eyes were completely grey and bloodshot and there were great bags of skin under her eyes.

Kattrinna had sunk into a chair and sat with her hands tightly clasped in her lap to stop them shaking. She was thinking of the radiant young eighteen-year-old in her red dress. That was the vision that had lived in her memory until now. She wondered whether she could ever bring herself to feel happy that Klara had come home.

'You should have written,' Kattrinna said. 'You should at least have sent us a message so we knew you were alive.'

'I know, I know,' her daughter said. And her voice at least was the same happy and bright voice as before. 'But I fell into bad ways at the start ... I suppose you may have heard?'

'Yes, we know that much,' Kattrinna said with a sigh.

'That's why I put off writing,' Klara said and gave a little laugh. There was something strong and competent about her, just as before. She certainly wasn't one of those women plagued with regret and soul-searching.

'Don't think about that now, Mother!' she said when Kattrinna still said nothing. 'Things are going really well now. I'm in charge of a restaurant now. Well, what I mean is I look after the meals on a big steamer that runs between Malmö and Lübeck. And this autumn I've rented a flat in Malmö. I did think of writing, but it was difficult to get started. Then I thought it could wait until the time came when I could fetch you and Father to me. And once I'd got everything ready, it seemed better to come and collect you myself rather than write.'

'You didn't hear anything about us then?' Kattrinna said. Klara's news ought to have made her happy, but she felt as despondent as before.

'No,' Klara answered, and then added apologetically: 'But I knew you'd get help if things became too bad.'

Then she must have noticed that Kattrinna's hands were trembling even though she was clenching them tight. She realised that times had treated them more harshly than she had imagined, and she tried to explain herself: 'I didn't want to send small sums of money home in the way other people do. I wanted to save until I could get a real home and bring you to join me.'

'It wasn't money we needed,' Kattrinna said. 'If you'd written, it would have been enough for us.'

Klara tried to rouse her mother from her melancholy frame of mind as she had done in the past.

'You mustn't spoil this moment for me, Mother!' she said. 'I'm here again now. Come, let's bring in my trunks and unpack them. There's food in them. Let's get a feast ready for Father coming home.'

She went outside to help unload her luggage from the gig, but Kattrinna did not follow her.

Klara had not asked about her father. She assumed that nothing had changed and that he still went to work at Falla Farm as before. Kattrinna knew that she had to tell her how things stood, but she kept putting it off. In spite of everything their little girl had brought a breath of fresh air to the cottage and Kattrinna hesitated to cut short her joy at returning home.

While Klara was helping unload the gig she noticed six or seven children coming to the gate and looking into the yard. They didn't say anything, they just laughed, pointed at her and ran away.

A few moments later they were back, but this time they

were accompanied by a little old man. He was yellow and wizened, but he walked erect with his head thrown back and his feet striking the ground firmly, like a soldier on the march.

'That's a strange creature, that one,' Klara said to the driver of the gig as the old man and the crowd of children came through the gate. She had no idea who it was, but she couldn't fail to notice a man in such splendid apparel. On his head he had a tall leather cap with a long plume and round his neck and right down over his chest hung crosses and stars cut from stiff, gold card and linked into chains. It looked as if he was wearing a ruff of gold.

The children were no longer silent, they were shouting, 'Empress, empress!' at the top of their voices. The old man made no effort to silence them and he marched forward as if the screaming, laughing gang of children were his guard of honour.

When the crowd was almost at the door of the cottage, Klara cried out and fled in to Kattrinna.

'Who is that?' she said, with a look of utter horror. 'Is that Father? Has he gone mad?'

'Yes,' Kattrinna said, so upset that the tears flowed and she hid her face in her apron.

'Because of me?'

'Our Lord in his mercy made him so. He saw that things were too hard for him to bear,' Kattrinna said.

She had no time to explain further because Jan was now in the doorway, accompanied by the crowd of children, who wanted to witness how this meeting, which had been described to them so often, would pass off in reality.

The Emperor of Portugallia did not go right up to his daughter. He came to a halt just inside the door and delivered his words of welcome:

'Welcome, welcome, to thee Klara,
To thee Fina, to thee rich Goldenborg!'

He uttered these words with the deliberate dignity shown by men of high rank on great occasions, but his eyes were full of tears of real joy and he found it hard to stop his voice trembling.

After declaiming this mighty welcome, the result of so much thought, the emperor struck the floor three times with his imperial cane to call for silence and attention and then he began to sing in a thin, shrill voice.

Klara had moved close to Kattrinna. She seemed to want to hide, to slip away behind her mother. She had said nothing so far, but when Jan raised his voice and began to sing, she shouted in horror and wanted to stop him.

But Kattrinna took hold of her arm in a tight grip.

'Let him be! He has been looking forward to singing this song to you ever since you went away.'

So she stood there in silence and let Jan continue.

This is the heartfelt happiness
Of the father of the Empress.
As the newspapers all have it.
Austria, Portugal,
Metz, Japan, as it was.
Boom, boom, boom and roll
Boom, boom.

But Klara could take no more. She leapt forward, quickly drove the children out and closed the door behind them.

Then she turned to her father and stamped her foot on the floor in rage. She was seriously angry.

'Stop that, will you, for Heaven's sake!' she said. 'Calling me empress! Are you trying to make a complete fool of me?'

Jan looked crestfallen, but it passed in an instant. She was, after all, the great empress! Everything she did was well done. Everything she said was honey and balsam. In his joy he had quite forgotten to look for her golden crown and golden throne and her captains dressed in gold. But if she chose to look poor and helpless when she came, that was her business. She had come back to him and that was joy enough.

Flight

One morning eight days after Klara's homecoming she and her mother were waiting at Borg Landing ready to leave forever. Old Kattrinna was wearing a hat and a fine coat. She was accompanying her daughter to Malmö where she was to become a respectable townswoman. Never again would she have to toil for her daily bread. She would sit on a sofa, her hands crossed in her lap, and for the rest of her days her life would be calm and untroubled.

But in spite of all the good things awaiting her, Kattrinna had never felt as deeply unhappy as she did now, standing there on the landing stage. Klara must have noticed something because she began to ask her mother whether she was afraid of the water. She then began to explain that there was no danger even though the wind was so strong that people were finding it almost impossible to remain on the landing stage. Klara was used to the sea, of course, so she knew what she was talking about. 'These are nothing like real waves!' she said to her mother. 'The water may be foaming white, but I still wouldn't be afraid to row across this lake in our old skiff.'

Klara ignored the storm and stayed out on the landing stage. Kattrinna, however, to avoid being blown away, went into the big warehouse and slipped into a dark corner behind some packing cases. She intended to stay there until the steamer arrived because she had no desire to meet any of the local people before she left. At the same time, however, she felt that behaving like this and being ashamed to be seen could never be right.

Whatever people might think, one thing she could not be accused of doing was leaving with Klara in order to have a life of luxury. She was going because her hands were failing her, and what else was there for her to do when she knew they were becoming so bad that she would be unable to do her spinning?

She saw Cantor Svartling come into the warehouse and she prayed to the Lord that he wouldn't see her and come over to ask where she was off to. How was she to tell him that she was leaving Jan and the cottage and her old life?

She had tried to arrange things so that she and Jan could carry on living at Skrolycka. If Klara would just agree to send them a little money, ten riksdaler a month perhaps, they would have been able to manage more or less. But there was no talking to Klara, she wouldn't listen: she wouldn't give them a penny unless Kattrinna came with her.

Kattrinna did understand Klara's position. Klara wasn't refusing out of unkindness. She had rented rooms and set things up for both parents. She had looked forward to the time she could show them she had been thinking of them and working for them. And she wanted to have at least one of them with her as a reward for her efforts.

It was almost certainly Jan she had had in mind when setting up her home, because she had been particularly close to him in the old days. But she thought it impossible to take him with her as he was.

The source of all the trouble was that Klara had formed such an aversion to her father that she simply could not have anything to do with him. She wouldn't let him talk to her about Portugallia, she wouldn't let him talk to her about her wealth and power, and she could scarcely bear seeing him dressed in his imperial apparel. He, however, was as happy with her as ever and constantly wanted to be close to her. But she fled from his presence and Kattrinna was sure that the reason their daughter refused to stay at home for more than a week was to avoid having to see him.

Klara came into the warehouse. She was not afraid of Cantor Svartling and without any hesitation she went over to speak to him. The very first thing she did was to tell him she was on her way back to her own home and Kattrinna was going with her.

As was only to be expected, the cantor then asked what her father had to say about it. And as calmly as if she were talking to a stranger, Klara told him of the arrangements she had made for Jan. She had rented a room for him with Lisa, the daughter-in-law of the old net maker. After Ol Bengtsa's death Lisa had had a new house built and she had a spare room where Jan could live.

Cantor Svartling had the kind of face that only revealed as much as he wanted it to reveal, so it remained expressionless while he was talking to Klara. But he was like a father to everyone in the parish and Kattrinna knew what he would be thinking. 'Why should an old man whose wife and daughter are still alive need to move in with strangers? Lisa is a kind soul, but she can't be expected to be as patient with him as his own family.' That's what he would be thinking. And he would be right to think it.

Kattrinna glanced quickly down at her hands. Was she just deceiving herself when she put the blame on them? Perhaps the real reason she was deserting Jan was that her daughter was too forceful and she was unable to stand up to her.

Klara was still talking to the cantor, telling him how they'd had to slip away from the cottage so that Jan wouldn't find out they were leaving.

That, for Kattrinna, had been the worst part of all. Klara had sent Jan off on an errand to a country store at the other end of the parish of Bro and as soon as he had gone they'd packed the trunks and left. Kattrinna had felt like a thief. Creeping away from home like that seemed criminal, but Klara said they had no choice. If Jan had known anything of their travel plans he would have lain down in front of the cart and let it run him over rather than allow them to go. As it was, Lisa would be there waiting for him when he arrived home. Kattrinna was sure she would try to comfort him, but it hurt to think how badly he would take it when he discovered that Klara had left him.

Cantor Svartling listened to Klara in silence, so much so that Kattrinna began to wonder whether he accepted what he was hearing. But then, suddenly he took Klara's hand and spoke to her in an earnest voice.

'As your old teacher, Klara, I'm going to be blunt and speak my mind. You want to run away from your duty, but there is no guarantee you will succeed. I have seen others try to do the same and it has brought its own punishment.'

Kattrinna stood up and gave a sigh of relief when she heard this. These were the very words she would have liked to address to her daughter.

Klara answered meekly enough that she could not think of any other way. She could not take a madman with her to a strange city and she herself could not stay here in Svartsjö. Jan had seen to that! Whenever she walked past a farm, children came running out shouting 'Empress' at her. And at church last Sunday people had been so eager to see her that they had almost knocked her over.

But the cantor still held firmly to his view.

'I recognise it may be difficult,' he said, 'but there has always been such a close relationship between you and your father. Don't imagine you can sever it so easily.'

Then the two of them left the warehouse and Kattrinna followed. She had changed her mind and now she wanted to talk to the cantor, but before approaching him she turned to look up the hill. She had a feeling that Jan would soon be there.

'Are you afraid Father will come?' Klara asked, leaving the cantor and walking over to her mother.

'Afraid?' Kattrinna said. 'I pray to God that he will get here in time. Before I leave.'

She summoned up all her courage and said: 'Do you know something? I feel I am doing something very wicked. I believe I shall suffer for it for the rest of my life.'

'You are just saying that because you've had to live in darkness and misery for so many years,' Klara said. 'It will be different once you are well and truly away from here. And, anyway, Father can't possibly get here because he doesn't know that we've left.'

'You shouldn't be too sure of that,' Kattrinna said. 'Jan

knows whatever he needs to know. He has been like that ever since you left us and as the years go by he knows more and more. Our Lord seems to have decided that since he has lost his mind he should be given a new light to guide him.'

Kattrinna now told Klara briefly about Lars Gunnarsson's death and the other events of recent years that proved that Jan had second sight, as it was called. Klara listened to her closely. Previously, whenever Kattrinna had tried to tell her how kind Jan was to many poor old souls, Klara had not wanted to listen.

Klara seemed so taken by this that Kattrinna began to hope she had started to see Jan in a different light and might even come home with her. It was not a hope she was allowed for long, for Klara suddenly exclaimed in a happy voice: 'Look, Mother, here comes the steamer! Fortune is with us and we can be on our way.'

Tears came to Kattrinna's eyes as the steamer drew alongside the landing stage. She had been intending to ask Cantor Svartling to speak to Klara on behalf of herself and Jan, hoping to convince Klara to let them stay in their old home. But there was no time now. She could see no way of avoiding this journey.

The steamer was running late and was in a great hurry to be on its way. They didn't even bother to put out the gangway and a couple of unfortunate passengers who wanted to disembark were thrown almost bodily up onto the landing stage by the crew. Klara took Kattrinna by the arm, a crewman caught her and she was on board. She was weeping and wanted to go back, but there was no mercy.

As Kattrinna arrived on board, Klara put an arm around her as if to steady her. 'Let's go over to the other side!' she said.

But it was too late. The old woman could see a man running down the hill and she immediately recognised who it was.

'There's Jan!' she said. 'What on earth will he do now?'

Jan halted on the end of the landing stage and stood there, small and pathetic. He saw Klara on the departing steamer and it is impossible to imagine a face that expressed more despair and grief than his did at that moment.

But the sight of Jan was all it took for Kattrinna to begin resisting her daughter. 'You can leave if you want to,' she said, 'but I'm getting off at the next landing place and going home.'

'You must do what you want to, Mother,' Klara said sadly, realising she could do nothing to stop her. And perhaps she, too, thought they had been too cruel to her father.

They were given no time to make redress. Not wanting to lose the joy of his life for a second time, Jan took a great leap from the landing stage and threw himself into the lake.

It's possible he had been intending to swim to the steamer, or it may have been that he felt life was no longer bearable.

People on the landing stage shouted, a boat was launched immediately and the little cargo steamer sent out its dinghy, but Jan had sunk. He did not come to the surface, not even once.

His imperial cane and the green leather cap were floating on the water, but the emperor himself had disappeared so silently and without trace that had these treasures not been there one would scarcely believe he was gone.

Detained

People thought it very odd that Klara Goldie from Skrolycka felt compelled to stay on Borg landing stage day after day waiting for someone who never came.

The days of her waiting were not the sweet days of summer, but the days of dark and stormy November and dark and cold December. Nor did she have lovely dreams of travellers from afar who would step ashore in pomp and splendour. She only had eyes and thoughts for a boat that was rowing back and forth across the lake, out beyond the landing stage, dragging for a drowned man. At first she had believed that once the dragging started the man she was seeking would be found immediately, but that did not happen. Two old fishermen worked the drag patiently day after day, but they could find nothing.

There were said to be deep holes in the bottom of the lake close to Borg Landing and many people thought Jan had sunk into one of them. Others said there was a strong current around the headland and it ran on out into the expanse of Kyrkviken Bay. He had perhaps been carried out there. Klara had the draglines extended so they could reach down to the deepest parts of Lake Löven, and she had every foot of Kyrkviken Bay dragged, but she failed to bring her father back up to the light of day.

Klara had ordered a coffin the very next day after the accident and when it was ready she had it brought to the landing stage so that she had a shelter for the dead man the moment he was found. She kept it on the landing stage, refusing even to put it in the warehouse, because the warehouse was locked when the factor left the landing place.

The coffin always had to be ready so that Jan would not have to wait.

The old emperor had often been surrounded by good friends on the landing stage and they had helped the time to pass, but Klara was almost always alone. She spoke to no one and people preferred to leave her to herself. In their eyes there was something uncanny about this woman who had been the cause of her father's death.

All traffic on the lake ceased in December and after that Klara had the landing stage to herself. No one disturbed her. The fishermen, who were still searching out on the lake, wanted to stop, but Klara became desperate. Her only hope and salvation lay in her father being found. As long as the lake refused to give him up, they must continue searching. They were to search around Nygård Point and Storvik Head, they were to search the whole of Lake Löven!

As for Klara herself, with every passing day she became more and more frantic to find the dead man. She had taken lodgings with one of the Borg crofters and at first she had gone there for an hour or so each day. But bit by bit her anguish grew and barely allowed her time to eat and sleep. She spent the whole time on the landing stage, staying there not only through the short winter days but during the long evenings until it was time to go to bed.

Old Kattrinna waited for Jan at Klara's side for the first two days after his death, but then she went home to Skrolycka.

It wasn't indifference that led her to leave the landing place, but she could no longer bear being with her daughter and listening to her talk about Jan. Klara made no attempt at pretence and Kattrinna knew that it was not tender solicitude or pangs of conscience that made Klara so eager to see his body resting in consecrated ground. It was because she was terrified, utterly terrified, as long as the man of whose death she was guilty lay unburied on the bottom of the lake. Once her father was interred in the soil of a churchyard, he would no longer be such a threat to her. But as long as he lay where he lay, he and the punishment he could call down upon her filled her with indescribable horror.

*

Klara stood on the landing stage at Borg looking down into the lake which, as always, was grey and restless. Her eyes could not penetrate beyond the surface, but she nevertheless thought she could see the bottom of the lake spreading into the distance beneath her.

Down there sat the Emperor of Portugallia. He was sitting on a rock, his hands around his knees, his eyes staring at the grey-green water, and he was waiting – constantly waiting – for her to join him.

He had lost his imperial regalia. The cane and the leather cap had not followed him to the depths, and the waters of the lake must have dissolved his paper stars. He sat there in an old coat, shiny with wear, and his hands were empty. But there was no longer anything false or ridiculous about him: now he was powerful and terrifying.

He had not been wrong when he said he was an emperor. In life, his power had been so great that the enemy he hated had been cast down and his friends had been helped. And he still possessed that power; it did not desert him because he was dead.

There had only ever been two people who had hurt him. He had already avenged himself on one of them. She was the other one – the daughter who had first driven him mad and then caused his death. He was waiting for her down there in the deep.

His love for her was over. He was no longer waiting to bestow praise and honour on her. He wanted to bring her to death's dark vale as a punishment for her crimes against him.

*

Something was calling Klara Goldie, she knew that. She wanted to lift the big, heavy lid of the coffin and launch it into the lake like a boat. She would climb down into it, push off from the lakeside and then carefully stretch out on the bed of sawdust.

She did not know whether it would sink immediately or whether she would drift around the lake for a while until the movement of the waves eventually filled her vessel and took it down to the deep.

She thought, too, that perhaps it wouldn't sink and she would be carried across the lake and washed ashore on one of the headlands fringed with alders.

It was such a temptation. She would lie quite still the whole time, not moving at all. She would not use her arms and hands to guide the coffin, she would leave everything to her judge. She would let him take her to him or allow her to escape, whichever he wanted.

If she submitted to his will, perhaps his great love might find its voice once more and he would take pity on her and pardon her.

But her terror was too great. She no longer dared rely on his love. She would never dare launch the black coffin into the lake.

*

An old friend and acquaintance of Klara Goldie came down to see her in these days. His name was August and he still lived at his parental home Där Nol in Prästerud.

He was a wise and calm man and talking to him helped her. He said she should leave and return to her old job. It was not good for her to stay here at the lonely landing place waiting for a dead man. She answered that she didn't dare depart before her father was buried in consecrated ground, but he wouldn't listen to that kind of talk.

Nothing was decided the first time he spoke to her, but the following time she promised to take his advice. They parted and he said he would return with his horse and carriage the following day and drive her to the railway station.

Had he done so, things would perhaps have passed off well. But he was prevented from coming himself and he sent his farm boy instead. She climbed into the carriage, anyway, and they set off. On the way she began talking to the driver about her father and she encouraged him to tell stories of her father's second sight. They were the same stories as Kattrinna had told her at the landing place, and there were others too.

After listening for a while, she asked the boy to turn back. Hearing the stories had frightened her so badly she didn't dare continue: the old Emperor of Portugallia was too powerful. She was well aware that the dead, unless buried in consecrated earth, may persecute and harry their enemies. She had to raise her father from the lake and lay him in the coffin. Until the words of God were read over him, she would not be granted a moment's peace.

Words of Farewell

Towards Christmas Klara received news that Kattrinna was dying. This, at last, was enough to drag her away from the landing place.

She walked home, as that was the best form of travel for anyone making for Askedalarna, and she took the usual old road through Lobyn and then up above the forest and the slopes of Storsnipa.

As she was passing the farm in Lobyn where old Björn Hindriksson had lived, she saw a big, sturdy, serious-looking man mending a fence by the roadside. He greeted her with a brief nod as she walked past, but then he stopped what he was doing and watched her, before finally hurrying to catch up.

'You are Klara Goldie from Skrolycka, aren't you?' he said. 'I need to have a few words with you. I'm Linnart, the son of Björn Hindriksson,' he added when he saw that she had no idea who he was.

'I'm very short of time,' Klara said, 'so perhaps we can talk another time? I've been told that my mother is dying.'

Linnart Björnsson suggested that he walk with her for a while. He had intended several times to come to the landing place to talk to her and he did not want to miss this opportunity. He thought it was important for her to hear what he had to say.

Klara made no objection. She noticed, however, that the man was finding it difficult to get round to what he wanted to say, so she did not expect it to be anything good. He cleared his throat several times and sought for the right words.

'I don't think you know, Klara, that I was the last person to speak to your father – the emperor, as we used to call him.'

Klara answered that she had not known that. At the same time she quickened her pace, no doubt thinking that this conversation was one she would prefer to avoid.

'I was out in the yard one day last autumn harnessing the horse ready for a trip to the store,' Linnart Björnsson continued, 'when I saw the emperor coming running down the road. It was obvious he was in a great hurry, but he stopped when he saw me to ask if the empress had gone past. I couldn't deny it, of course, and he burst into floods of tears. He said he'd been on the way to Bro but he'd been overwhelmed by such a feeling of anxiety that he had turned back. When he arrived home, the cottage was empty. Kattrinna had gone too. They must have been going to the steamer and he simply didn't know how he would get to Borg Landing before they departed.'

Klara stopped abruptly. 'I see, so you gave him a lift?' she said.

'Yes,' the farmer said. 'Jan did me a great service many years ago and I wanted to repay him. But perhaps helping him on his way wasn't such a good deed after all?'

'Oh no,' Klara said. 'The fault is all mine. I should never have tried to run away from him.'

'He was crying like a child the whole time he was in my cart,' Linnart Björnsson said, 'and I had no idea what to say to comfort him, so I just kept quiet. Eventually I said, "I think we'll make it, Jan. Don't cry – these small boats that run in the autumn are not known for speed." No sooner had I said that than he put his hand on my arm and asked me whether I thought the people who'd kidnapped the empress would treat her harshly.'

'The people who'd kidnapped me!' Klara repeated in amazement.

'I was as amazed as you are, Klara Goldie, and I asked him who he meant. Well, apparently he meant all the people who'd been waiting to ambush the empress while she was at home. All the enemies she had been so afraid of that she hadn't dared wear her golden crown or as much as mention Portugallia. And now they had captured her and were carrying her off as a prisoner.'

'Ah, so that's what he thought!'

'Yes, that's just what he thought, Klara,' Linnart said, emphasising his words. 'You must understand that your father wasn't crying because he had been left alone, but because he thought you were in danger.'

These last words stuck in Linnart Björnsson's throat and he found it difficult to get them out. Perhaps he was remembering old Björn Hindriksson and himself. There were things in his own story that meant that he understood the value we should put on a love that never fails.

But Klara Goldie still did not understand. Ever since arriving home she had thought of her father with nothing but fear and distaste. She muttered something to herself about her father being a fool.

Linnart Björnsson heard what she said and it wounded him. 'I don't know whether Jan really was so crazy,' he said. 'I told him that I hadn't seen any guards around Klara Goldie and he replied: "Dear Linnart, did you not see how they kept watch on her as she travelled past. Pride was there and Harshness, Lust was there and Vice, all the enemies she had to combat in her realm."'

Klara stopped and turned to him: 'Well?' That was all she said.

'I answered that I, too, had seen those enemies!' Linnart Björnsson said grimly.

Klara gave a laugh.

'But I immediately regretted having said that,' the farmer went on, 'because Jan began to cry again, despairingly. "Oh, please pray to God, dear Linnart, that I can save my little girl from all evil. It doesn't matter what happens to me, as long as she is helped."'

Klara said nothing and quickened her pace even more. Something was beginning to tear at her heart, but she forced it to remain silent and still. If it broke loose, she did not know how she would bear it.

'Well, those were his words of farewell, I suppose,' Linnart Björnsson said. 'And shortly after that he showed that he meant what he said. You must not believe, Klara, that Jan leapt into the lake to escape his own sorrows. He threw himself into the lake behind the steamer trying to save you from your enemies.'

Klara Goldie rushed along faster and faster. All her father's love from first to last began to reveal itself to her, and she wanted to flee from it. The knowledge was more than she could endure.

'We take far too little care of one another in this parish,' Linnart continued, keeping up with her without any effort. 'There was a good deal of resentment against you, Klara Goldie, after the emperor drowned. And, for my part, I didn't consider you worthy to hear his last words and thoughts. But we have changed our minds. We like you staying down there on the landing stage and waiting for him.'

Klara came to a halt. Her cheeks were red and her eyes glinted with rage.

'I only stay there because I'm afraid of him,' she said.

'You have never pretended to be better than you are. We know that, Klara. But perhaps we understand better than you do yourself what lies behind this waiting. We, too, have had parents. And we, too, have not always treated them properly.'

Klara Goldie was so angry that she wanted to say something dreadful, but nothing came out. She wanted to stamp her foot and make him hold his tongue, but she was unable to do that either. She saw no other course open to her than to turn on her heel and run.

Linnart Björnsson did not follow. He had said what he wanted to say and he was not displeased with his morning's work.

Kattrinna's Death

When Klara entered the little cottage at Skrolycka Kattrinna was lying in bed, deathly pale and with her eyes closed. It looked as if the end had already come.

But as soon as Klara was standing beside her stroking her hand, she looked up and began to speak.

'Jan wants me to be with him,' she said with a great effort. 'He doesn't blame me for leaving him.'

Klara gave a start. She began to understand why her mother was dying. She had been a faithful wife all her life and betraying Jan at the end had broken her heart.

'You mustn't blame yourself!' Klara said. 'I was the one who forced you to leave.'

'It's been very hard to think about it,' Kattrinna said. 'But everything is good and well between us now.'

She shut her eyes again and lay quite still. A faint glow of happiness seemed to spread across her worn face.

But she soon began talking again. There were things that needed to be said and that she needed to say in order to find rest: 'Don't be angry with Jan for running after you. He only wanted what was best for you. You had a difficult time after the two of you parted, he knew that. And he had a hard time too. Both of you got lost – each in your own way.'

Klara Goldie had known her mother would say something of this kind and she had steeled herself in advance. But what her mother was saying moved her more than she had expected and she tried to give her a good answer.

'I shall think of Father as he was in the old days,' she said. 'You must remember what good friends we always were?'

Kattrinna seemed satisfied with her answer, for she lay back peacefully again. She had probably not intended to say more, but all of a sudden she gave her daughter a smile filled with love.

'I am so happy that you've got your beauty back again, Klara,' she said.

Her smile and her words shattered Klara's self-control and she fell to her knees beside the low bed and began to weep. For the first time since her return home she really wept.

'I don't know how you can still be like this, Mother. It is my fault that you are dying, and I am guilty of my father's death too.'

Kattrinna was still smiling and she stroked her daughter gently.

'You are so good, Mother, you are so good to me,' Klara said through her tears.

Kattrinna took a firm hold of her hand and pulled herself up in bed to deliver her final testimony. She said: 'Everything that is good in me, I have learnt from Jan.'

Then she sank back and said nothing more that was audible or lucid. The work of dying started and she died the following morning.

Klara Goldie lay on the floor beside the bed and wept as her mother fought her death struggle. She lay there the whole time, weeping away her anguish, her feverish dreams, her burden of guilt. Her tears had no end.

The Emperor's Funeral

The funeral of Kattrinna from Skrolycka was to take place on the Sunday before Christmas. There are not usually many people at church on that day because most people want to save their churchgoing for the great festivals.

But when the small cortège from Askedalarna arrived at the gathering place between the church and the parish hall, they were taken aback. Such a great crowd of people as was present that day had scarcely ever been seen there, not even, for instance, when the old dean from Bro came to give his annual sermon in Svartsjö, or when a new minister was being selected.

It scarcely needs to be said that all these people would not have come to the graveside of old Kattrinna, so some other event was obviously happening. It's possible they were expecting some grand figure to be attending church that day, or perhaps the sermon was to be given by a different minister, someone other than the usual one? Askedalarna was so isolated that news of many of the things happening in the parish never reached its residents.

The funeral party drove up as usual to the space behind the parish hall and the people stepped out of the carriages. It was as crowded there as it had been at the front but, apart from that, they couldn't see anything out of the ordinary. They did, however, begin to wonder about it, though they refrained from asking anyone what was going on: people in a funeral party tend to keep themselves to themselves and not start chatting to those who aren't mourners.

Kattrinna's coffin was taken from the open-sided wagon which had carried it to the church and placed on two black trestles set up outside the parish hall. It would wait there, along with the mourners, until the bells began to ring and the minister and the cantor were ready to accompany it to the churchyard.

The weather was unrelentingly awful. Rain was lashing down and rattling on the lid of the coffin. One thing was certain: whatever it was that had brought all these church folk together, it wasn't the weather.

On this particular day, however, it seemed that no one bothered about the rain and the wind. Silently and patiently they all stood out in the open, without seeking shelter in the church or the parish hall.

The six bearers and the mourners who were gathered around Kattrinna noticed that in addition to the trestles on which Kattrinna's coffin lay, a second pair had been set up. So there was to be another burial. They hadn't heard of this happening before. And there was no sign yet of the approach of another funeral party which, given the time, should already have arrived at the church.

When the clock stood at ten minutes to ten and the time to be moving to the churchyard was fast approaching, the people from Askedalarna noticed that everyone else was moving towards the farm Där Nol in Prästerud, which lay just a few minutes from the church.

They hadn't noticed before, but now they saw that spruce twigs were scattered all the way from the parish hall to the farmhouse and that a spruce tree had been placed on each side of the front door. That, then, was where there had been a death, though they could not understand how they hadn't heard anything about someone dying at such an important farm. Nor were there any sheets hanging in the windows, as there ought to be when a house is in mourning.

Just then the front door opened wide and a funeral procession emerged. First came August Där Nol carrying the funeral staff and wreath in his hand, and he was followed by the bearers with the coffin.

The crowd of people who had been waiting outside the church joined this procession. This was the death that had brought them here.

They carried the coffin to the parish hall and put it down to the right of the coffin that was already there. August Där Nol moved the trestles so that the two coffins would be right beside one another.

The coffin that had just arrived was neither as new nor as clean as Kattrinna's. It looked as if it had been scoured by many rainstorms before this day. And it had been treated roughly and was chipped and scratched.

All the Askedalarna people gave a great sigh, all at the same moment, for now they were beginning to understand. This coffin did not contain one of August Där Nol's kinsmen, nor had all of these people come to the church for the sake of some visiting dignitary.

All eyes went to Klara Goldie to see if she understood, and they could see at once that she did.

Pale and with her eyes swollen from weeping, she had been standing beside her mother's coffin the whole time, but when she recognised the other coffin which the bearers carried from Där Nol Farm, she looked overwhelmed by the joy that comes from receiving at last what she had long sought. But she calmed herself quickly, smiled a smile of sorrow and gently stroked the lid of the coffin. It was as if she wanted to say to her dead mother: 'Now you have everything you would ever have desired.'

August Där Nol came over to Klara and took her hand.

'I hope you have no objections to us doing it this way?' he said. 'We only found him on Friday and I thought this would make it easier for you, Klara.'

Klara answered with few words, her lips trembling so much that they were barely audible.

'Thank you, it's fine. I know he is coming to Mother, not to me.'

'I'm sure that you'll come to understand that he is coming to both of you, Klara,' August said.

The old widow from Falla Farm, eighty years old and bowed by sorrows, had come to the church to honour Kattrinna, who had been her faithful servant and friend for many years.

With her she had brought the imperial cane and cap that had been returned to her. Her intention had been to place them in Kattrinna's grave, thinking she would like something to remind her of Jan.

Klara Goldie went to her now and asked for the imperial treasure and then she leaned the cane on Jan's coffin and hung the cap on the cane. Everyone understood what she was thinking: since coming home she had refused to allow Jan to wear his imperial finery and now she wanted to make what recompense she could. There is not much one can do for the dead.

No sooner was the cane there than the bell in the church tower began to ring and the minister and the cantor and the verger came out of the vestry and took their places at the head of the procession.

The rain was coming in squalls that day, but fortunately there was a break now as the congregation formed ranks, men first and then womenfolk, to accompany Jan and Kattrinna to the churchyard.

The people forming the procession appeared somehow surprised to be there. They were not exactly in mourning, nor were they present to show particular honour to either of the dead. It was just that when the news spread through the parish that Jan from Skrolycka had been found in time to be laid in the same grave as Kattrinna, everyone thought there was something remarkable and beautiful about it. They had all wanted to attend and see the old couple reunited in death.

None of them could have expected so many others to have the same thought. It was almost as if too much fuss was being made for two poor and humble folk. People were looking at one another slightly shamefacedly, but now that they were there the only thing to do was to go to the churchyard.

And they had to smile to themselves when they thought how much the Emperor of Portugallia would have liked it. Two staffbearers – for the Askedalarna people had one too, of course – walked in front of his and Kattrinna's coffins and almost everyone in the parish was in the procession that followed them. It could not have been better if the emperor himself had been able to arrange it.

And we cannot be absolutely certain that it wasn't all his work after all. The old emperor had become remarkable after his death, he really had. He must have had something in mind when he made his daughter wait and wait, and again when he rose from the deep at just the right time. There must surely have been something behind it.

After the coffins had been lowered into the wide grave, the cantor began to sing: 'I walk the darkest valley ...'

Cantor Svartling was an old man by this time and his song reminded Klara of another old man's song, to which she had been unwilling to listen.

The memory caused her great pain. She pressed her hands to her heart and closed her eyes to stop them betraying her suffering.

Standing there with her eyes closed she saw her father as he had been in her childhood, when he and she had been such friends.

She saw again his face as she had seen it one morning when there had been a blizzard during the night and the snow on the road was so deep he had carried her to school.

She saw it, too, on the day she had gone to church in her red dress. No one, no one at all, could have looked as kind and as happy as he did then.

And then his happiness had come to an end, and she herself had never really been at peace since.

She struggled to keep his face before her eyes. It was good for her and a great wave of tenderness rose within her when she saw it.

It was a face that wanted nothing but her best. It wasn't a face to be afraid of.

It was just kind, old Jan at Skrolycka and he had no wish to sit in judgment or to sentence his only child to punishment and unhappiness.

She grew so calm. Now that she could see him again as he had been, she entered a world of loving kindness. How could she have believed he hated her. All he wanted was to forgive.

Wherever she went and wherever she stood, he had wanted

to be near her, to protect her. That was all he'd wanted.

Once again she felt a great wave of tenderness swell from her heart and fill her whole being. All at once she knew that everything was good again. She and her father were one, as they had been before. Now, now when she loved him, nothing more was needed, there was nothing more to be atoned for.

Klara woke as from a dream. While she had been standing gazing on her father's good face, the minister had performed the burial service. Now he was addressing a few words to the congregation. He thanked them for attending this funeral in such great numbers. The man they were laying to rest here was not some great and noble figure, but he had possessed what was perhaps the warmest and richest heart in the parish.

When the minister said this the congregation looked at one another, this time with looks of satisfaction. The minister was right, this was what had brought them to the funeral.

Then he directed a few words to Klara. She had received greater love from her parents than anyone else he knew, and such love must be turned into a blessing.

As the minister said this all those present turned to look at Klara and they were filled with wonder at what they saw.

The minister's words seemed to have already come true. There she was, Klara Fina Goldenborg from Skrolycka, the girl who was named after the sun, standing at the grave of her parents and she shone like one transfigured.

She was as beautiful as the Sunday she went to church in the red dress, perhaps even more beautiful.

Translator's Afterword

In letters to her closest friends, Sophie Elkan and Valborg Olander, in February 1914, Selma Lagerlöf wrote that she was working on a major novel: 'I started it last autumn, but at that stage I had no idea what would happen in it. It was a real bother. But thanks to one of those flashes of inspiration it has become a pleasure to think about. Now it will be written, which is the most important thing.' The novel was *The Emperor of Portugallia*: 'The action takes place here in Emtervik when I was a child and all the usual old figures are present as background characters. The main character is real, too, a poor old fellow who was driven mad by grief for his daughter. In its own way it's a King Lear story.' In a later letter to her publisher Karl Otto Bonnier Lagerlöf apologises for creating yet another main character who is mad, but goes on to emphasise that he was a real figure: 'The impression he made on us children was never nasty or frightening and he was just a goldmine of fantasies and nice ideas.'

The writing was far from easy and Lagerlöf comments on several occasions how the political situation and the outbreak of war in August made it difficult to keep one's mind on work. At the end of May there was also a more positive cause of disruption when Selma Lagerlöf was elected as the first woman member of the Swedish Academy. Nevertheless, the novel was finished by the middle of November, including a substantial rethinking and rewriting of the final chapters on the advice of Valborg Olander: Lagerlöf's original plan had been to end the novel with a dramatic collision between two steamships on the lake. The novel, with illustrations by Albert Engström, was published in December 1914 and achieved immediate critical and popular acclaim.

*

The story opens with a scene with comic overtones in which Jan, a poor day labourer, is standing despondently in the rain outside his cottage while his wife Kattrinna is giving birth to their first and only child. The marriage lacks enthusiasm and Jan has no desire for a family, so he is mulling over all the disadvantages it will bring. But the moment his newborn daughter is put in his arms he is overwhelmed by feelings of love and joy he has never experienced before. As the child, Klara, grows, she and her father become ever closer. And Klara is a clever child, with an ability to solve problems and deal with situations well beyond her years.

Farmer Erik, Jan's employer, dies as a result of an accident in the forest after his son-in-law and heir Lars Gunnarsson purposely delays help reaching the injured man. On the pretext that Jan has never paid for the land on which his cottage stands, Gunnarsson threatens the family with eviction unless he receives 200 kronor before 1 October. Klara, now seventeen years old, offers to go to Stockholm, find work and earn the required sum. Reluctantly her parents agree, convinced of her ability to solve their problems. Before she leaves on the steamboat, Jan witnesses her surveying the wide world from the top of the nearby mountain and singing in joy at her coming departure.

Klara leaves for Stockholm at midsummer and during the following months her parents hear that she has found work, but when 1 October arrives and Klara has neither returned nor sent the money, Jan throws himself on his bed in a state of depression. Before the day is out, however, Karl Karlsson, a local politician, arrives with 200 kronor Klara has sent to him: she has asked him to pay the debt and to deal with the legal problems on her behalf. In her accompanying letter she says she is in the employ of a rich woman in Stockholm who has advanced her the money, which she must work off.

Since the debt has now been cleared, it is obvious that the

cause of Jan's continued depression is Klara's failure to return home, and he begins to imagine that she is communicating with him through others in the parish. He takes to visiting the landing stage by the lake, daily expecting Klara to return, but now rumours are spreading through the parish that Klara has become a prostitute in Stockholm. Jan protects himself against this knowledge by creating for Klara the role of Empress of Portugallia who, one day, will return home in all her glory. He, meanwhile, as her father, is the Emperor of Portugallia and he constantly parades the district in home-made regalia, insisting that everyone – including the local gentry – treat him in a manner appropriate to his new status.

Fifteen years pass before Klara returns home. She is dressed as an affluent city woman, but her beauty has gone and her face is marked with the coarse features of a sinful life. She has earned sufficient money to rent a flat in Malmö and has come home to fetch her mother and father to live with her. She is so shocked, however, by her father's decline into madness and his role as parish fool that she convinces Kattrinna to leave him and run away with her. On seeing them on the deck of the departing steamer, Jan hurls himself into the lake and drowns. Now it is Klara who cannot leave the landing place, fearful of the vengeance her father's spirit will wreak unless she can give his body a proper burial in consecrated earth. At last his body is found and, together with his wife Kattrinna, he is given an emotional funeral attended by the whole parish.

*

Henrik Wivel has described the novel as 'perhaps the most private of Selma Lagerlöf's books', and it may be that which accounts for the slight sense of unease a modern reader may feel at times – a sense of intruding into a relationship that carries within it the seeds of tragedy almost from the start. The core of the novel lies in the relationship of father and daughter, a relationship that, as we have seen, led Selma Lagerlöf in her letters to consider 'a Swedish King Lear' as a possible title, thus emphasising the work's potential for tragedy. Wivel also points out how frequently the motif of parent and child figures in Lagerlöf's work and he connects this with her own relationship with her family, and with her father in particular.

The novel presents us with a cycle: the birth of his daughter Klara, a child he had expected to bring nothing but toil and responsibility, creates a family and wakens Jan emotionally to life: 'he began to realise what had been wrong with him throughout his whole life. For someone who cannot feel the workings of sorrow and joy in his heart cannot yet be considered a real human being'. Initially the relationship between Jan and Klara is all joy as it deepens, seemingly idyllically, throughout Klara's childhood. For Jan, his love for, and pride in, Klara become an obsession that excludes all else, including his wife Kattrinna; he is even prepared to sacrifice his most valuable and symbolically most precious possession – his bridegroom's shirt – for the comfort of the child when she falls ill with scarlet fever. His obsessive love and pride is reinforced by the opinions voiced by other characters: 'that clever little girl of yours, she'll bring you joy, that one' or 'It would have been better for all of us if Klara had been in the Garden of Eden instead of Eve!'

The Emperor of Portugallia, then, is a novel that explores the family and the rights and duties in the relationship between parents and children. It has been described as 'a sermon on the fourth commandment' – 'Honour thy father and thy mother, as the Lord thy God has commanded thee'. In the chapter 'The Catechetical Meeting' the minister paints a picture of the perfect family in which generation after generation live together and the old are cared for and respected. The minister, however, does not address the converse – that is voiced by Ol Bengtsa to his son in the chapter 'The Sunday after Midsummer': 'I've no doubt you are sitting there thinking to yourself how strange it is that Our Lord failed to write a commandment telling parents how to behave towards their children'. Love for one's children can become a blind and unconscious assumption of ownership and it is this that leads to catastrophe for the family at Skrolycka. Jan fails to recognise the early signs of Klara's natural and legitimate desire for independence and for her own identity, he fails to read the import of her picking the apples or wearing the red dress or offering so promptly to earn the money necessary to save the cottage. Not until he witnesses her on the summit of Storsnipa, singing and gazing out over 'the grandeur, immensity and richness from which she had been excluded until this day,' does he understand that 'his little girl was not offering to save their cottage from love, but from a desire to go out into the world and leave them'.

This is where his madness begins, at first mildly, but then the depressive symptoms develop into full delusional psychosis and he creates for himself the role of Emperor of Portugallia. With gentle loyalty and wise understanding, Kattrinna tells us: 'Our Lord has put blinkers on him so he doesn't have to see the things he can't bear to see. We can be thankful for that.' His imperial madness, then, protects him from the truth he witnessed on the mountain, and it continues to protect him against the parish gossip that his daughter has become a prostitute. He goes to his death fifteen years later still believing he is trying to save Klara, his empress, from the evil forces that are attempting to abduct her.

The life lie that has enabled Jan to survive ultimately brings about his death. For him there is to be, it would seem, no redemption at the end of his *via dolorosa*. But as always in Selma Lagerlöf's writings there is both redemption and reconciliation. Jan's death and the revelation of the many small acts of kindness and goodwill he performed during his years of mad wandering bring Klara to an understanding of how much her father loved her and, in the words of the minister, that her father, for all his madness, possessed the warmest and richest heart in the parish. The final scene in the churchyard, the joint burial of Jan and Kattrinna, and Klara's reconciliation in death with both father and mother, completes the cycle: the novel begins with the creation of the family, the course of the novel sees the family shattered by obsessive love that leads to flight and to madness, and now the family is brought together once more.

*

In a recent essay on Selma Lagerlöf and cinema Anna Nordlund writes: 'Selma Lagerlöf's writing career coincided with the rise of the modern media, and she received a great deal of attention from the emerging new culture industry. The success of Swedish silent cinema depended to a considerable extent on adaptations of works by Lagerlöf and her texts provide an example of the important role that prose fiction played for the emerging film industry'.

Nordlund goes on to remind us that the cultural status of film was low and that it was frequently considered to be an unhealthy form of popular entertainment. Selma Lagerlöf's reputation and her willingness to be involved with the new medium contributed significantly to making early Swedish cinema a Golden Age and to bridging the divide between high and low culture.

In 1919 Selma Lagerlöf entered into an agreement with Svenska Bio giving the company the right to film her works. Twelve of her books were filmed, mainly by Victor Sjöström and Mauritz Stiller, the two leading directors of the day. Sjöström moved to Hollywood in 1923 and remained in America until 1930. While there he worked under the anglicised name of Seastrom and it was under that name that he directed the 1925 silent version of *Kejsarn av Portugallien* for Metro-Goldwyn-Mayer. The film was issued under the title *The Tower of Lies* and starred two of the biggest names of the Hollywood silent era, Lon Chaney and Norma Shearer. Unfortunately, apart from a few still photographs, the film has not survived. The MGM poster blurb states, slightly inaccurately, that: '*The Tower of Lies* is a powerful, heart-stirring drama based on Selma Lagerlöf's Nobel Prize novel *The Emperor of Portugallia*'. (The novel was written some five years after the award of the Nobel Prize.) Richard Watts Jr., writing in *Theatre Magazine*, December 1925, tells us that 'Lon Chaney's performance as the grief-crazed Jan is one of the most notable of recent screen portraits. He ceases to be a Hollywood actor and really becomes the poor old peasant'.

The film was released in Sweden in 1926 with the title *Kejsarn av Portugallien* and Selma Lagerlöf herself saw it at the cinema in Sunne, near her Mårbacka home. A six-minute short – *Ett besök hos Selma Lagerlöf* (A Visit to Selma Lagerlöf) – which shows her studying stills from the film and driving to the cinema can be viewed online at www.filmarkivet.se .

Two other film versions of the novel have been made since then: Gustaf Molander's 1944 *Kejsarn av Portugallien*, which had Victor Sjöström –an acclaimed actor as well as director – playing the part of Jan, and the 1992-93 TV mini-series *Kejsarn av Portugallien*, written and directed by Lars Molin. Molander's film was not well received by the critics as it was considered to take unnecessary liberties with the novel, not merely simplifying Lagerlöf's original but coarsening it. Molin's mini-series follows the novel faithfully and was given a much more positive reception.

*

Kejsarn av Portugallien was published in the autumn of 1914 and the speed with which translations of the novel began to appear testifies to Selma Lagerlöf's international reputation – it is tempting to say following her Nobel Prize of 1909 although, in fact, most of her earlier novels were made available to international audiences just as quickly. Finnish and Danish translations of the new novel were already available in 1914; German, Dutch and Russian versions followed in 1915; and an English translation came in 1916. All in all, the novel has been translated into thirty languages, in some cases a number of times. Virtually all the European languages are represented and farther afield we can find Turkish, Chinese and Japanese.

The sole English translation was made by Velma Swanston Howard: *The Emperor of Portugallia*, Garden City, New York: Doubleday, Page & Co., 1916. The same translation appeared in London in 1916, was republished in London and New York in 1917 and again in Los Angeles in 2005. Velma Swanston Howard (1868-1937), an American of Swedish origin, was by far the most prolific early translator of Lagerlöf's works and many of her translations have been repeatedly republished up to the present day. It is, perhaps, easy to be critical of Velma Swanston Howard's work by modern standards, but it would be difficult to overestimate the importance of her devotion to the cause of Selma Lagerlöf in the English-speaking world. Between 1908 and 1935 Swanston Howard and Selma Lagerlöf corresponded regularly and a collection of some 543 letters is held by the Swedish National Library in Stockholm. In a number of rewarding recent articles Björn Sundmark has studied the correspondence and thrown considerable light both on Lagerlöf's wishes and on Swanston Howard's working aims and practices. It is clear, in Sundmark's words, that Swanston Howard 'comes close to idolizing Lagerlöf', and, perhaps surprisingly, that she lacked self-confidence as a translator and had a tendency to over-revise. He quotes a letter in which Lagerlöf advises her not to overdo things: 'Isn't the simple English of your letters good enough?' The present translation has been made from the first edition of *Kejsarn av Portugallien* (Stockholm, Albert Bonniers förlag, 1914), accessed electronically through the Swedish Literature Bank (www. litteraturbanken.se).

This is the first of my translations in the Lagerlöf in English series to be made without the support of the late series editor Helena Forsås-Scott, who passed away in 2015; she is very much missed. My grateful thanks go to my friends and colleagues Sarah Death (who has taken over the general editorship) and Linda Schenck, both of whom provided useful and supportive advice and suggestions on more than just language issues. Thank you, too, to Janet Garton for her as always careful reading and to Marita Fraser, Essi Viitanen and Elettra Carbone for the great care and imagination they put into producing such elegant editions.

Further Reading:

Cullgren, Carina, 'Jan i Skrolycka – en far i fiktiv gestaltning,' in *I Selma Lagerlöfs värld (Lagerlöfstudier 2005)*, ed. Maria Karlsson and Louise Vinge. Stockholm/ Stehag: Brutus Östlings Bokförlag Symposion, 2005

Edström, Vivi, *Selma Lagerlöf*. Stockholm: Natur och Kultur, 1991.

Graves, Peter, 'The reception of Selma Lagerlöf in Britain', in *Selma Lagerlöf Seen From Abroad*, ed. Louise Vinge, Kungliga Vitterhets och Antikvitets Akademien, Konferenser 44, 1998.

Holm, Birgitta, *Selma Lagerlöf och ursprungets roman*. Stockholm: Norstedts, 1984.

Lagerlöf, Ulla-Britta, 'Selma Selmissima – en stark personlighet', *Parnass*, 1994, no. 5.

Nordlund, Anna, 'Selma Lagerlöf in the golden age of Swedish silent cinema,' in *Re-Mapping Lagerlöf: Performance, Intermediality and European Transmissions,* ed. Helena Forsås-Scott, Lisbeth Stenberg and Bjarne Thorup Thomsen. Lund: Nordic Academic Press, 2014.

Sundmark, Björn, '"Dear Selma" – "Dear Velma": Velma Swanston Howard's Letters to Selma Lagerlöf', in *Re-Mapping Lagerlöf: Performance, Intermediality and European Transmissions,* ed. Helena Forsås-Scott, Lisbeth Stenberg and Bjarne Thorup Thomsen. Lund: Nordic Academic Press, 2014.

Toijer-Nilsson, Ying (ed), *Du lär mig att bli fri: Selma Lagerlöf skriver till Sophie Elkan.* Stockholm: Albert Bonniers förlag, 1992.

Toijer-Nilsson, Ying (ed), *Mammas Selma: Selma Lagerlöfs brev till modern.* Stockholm: Albert Bonniers förlag, 1998.

Toijer-Nilsson, Ying (ed), *En riktig författarhustru: Selma Lagerlöf skriver till Valborg Olander.* Stockholm: Albert Bonniers förlag, 2006.

SELMA LAGERLÖF

Mårbacka

(translated by Sarah Death)

The property of Mårbacka in Värmland was where Selma Lagerlöf grew up, immersed in a tradition of storytelling. Financial difficulties led to the loss of the house, but Lagerlöf was later able to buy it back, rebuild and make it the centre of her world. The book *Mårbacka*, the first part of a trilogy written in 1922-32, can be read as many different things: memoir, fictionalised autobiography, even part of Lagerlöf's myth-making about her own successful career as an author. It is part social and family history, part mischievous satire in the guise of innocent, first-person child narration, part declaration of filial love.

Mårbacka
ISBN 9781909408296
UK £12.95
(Paperback, 270 pages)

SELMA LAGERLÖF

The Löwensköld Ring
Charlotte Löwensköld
Anna Svärd

(translated by Linda Schenck)

The Löwensköld Ring (1925) is the first volume of the trilogy considered to have been Selma Lagerlöf's last work of prose fiction. Set in the Swedish province of Värmland in the eighteenth century, the narrative traces the consequences of the theft of General Löwensköld's ring from his coffin, and develops into a disturbing tale of revenge from beyond the grave. It is also a tale about decisive women. The narrative twists and the foregrounding of alternative interpretations confront the reader with a pervasive sense of ambiguity. *Charlotte Löwensköld* (1925) is the story of the following generations, a tale of psychological insight and social commentary, and of the complexities of a mother-son relationship. How we make our life 'choices' and what evil forces can be at play around us is beautifully and ironically depicted and comes to a close in the third volume, *Anna Svärd* (1928).

The Löwensköld Ring
ISBN 9781870041928
UK £9.95
(Paperback, 120 pages)

Charlotte Löwensköld
ISBN 9781909408067
UK £11.95
(Paperback, 290 pages)

Anna Svärd
ISBN 9781909408289
UK £12.95
(Paperback, 330 pages)

SELMA LAGERLÖF

Nils Holgersson's Wonderful Journey through Sweden

(translated by Peter Graves)

Nils Holgersson's Wonderful Journey through Sweden (1906-07) is truly unique. Starting life as a commissioned school reader designed to present the geography of Sweden to nine-year-olds, it quickly won the international fame and popularity it still enjoys over a century later. The story of the naughty boy who climbs on the gander's back and is then carried the length of the country, learning both geography and good behaviour as he goes, has captivated adults and children alike, as well as inspiring film-makers and illustrators. The elegance of the present translation – the first full translation into English – is beautifully complemented by the illustrations specially created for the volume.

Nils Holgersson's Wonderful Journey through Sweden, Volume 1
ISBN 9781870041966
UK £12.95
(Paperback, 365 pages)

Nils Holgersson's Wonderful Journey through Sweden, Volume 2
ISBN 9781870041973
UK £12.95
(Paperback, 380 pages)

Nils Holgersson's Wonderful Journey through Sweden, The Complete Volume
ISBN 9781870041966
UK £29.95
(Hardback, 684 pages)

SELMA LAGERLÖF

The Phantom Carriage

(translated by Peter Graves)

Written in 1912, Selma Lagerlöf's *The Phantom Carriage* is a powerful combination of ghost story and social realism, partly played out among the slums and partly in the transitional sphere between life and death. The vengeful and alcoholic David Holm is led to atonement and salvation by the love of a dying Salvation Army slum sister under the guidance of the driver of the death-cart that gathers in the souls of the dying poor. Inspired by Charles Dickens's *A Christmas Carol*, *The Phantom Carriage* remained one of Lagerlöf's own favourites, and Victor Sjöström's 1920 film version of the story is one of the greatest achievements of the Swedish silent cinema.

The Phantom Carriage
ISBN 9781870041911
UK £11.95
(Paperback, 126 pages)